THE UNITED STATES AT WAR

THE PERSIAN GULF WAR AND THE WAR IN IRAQ

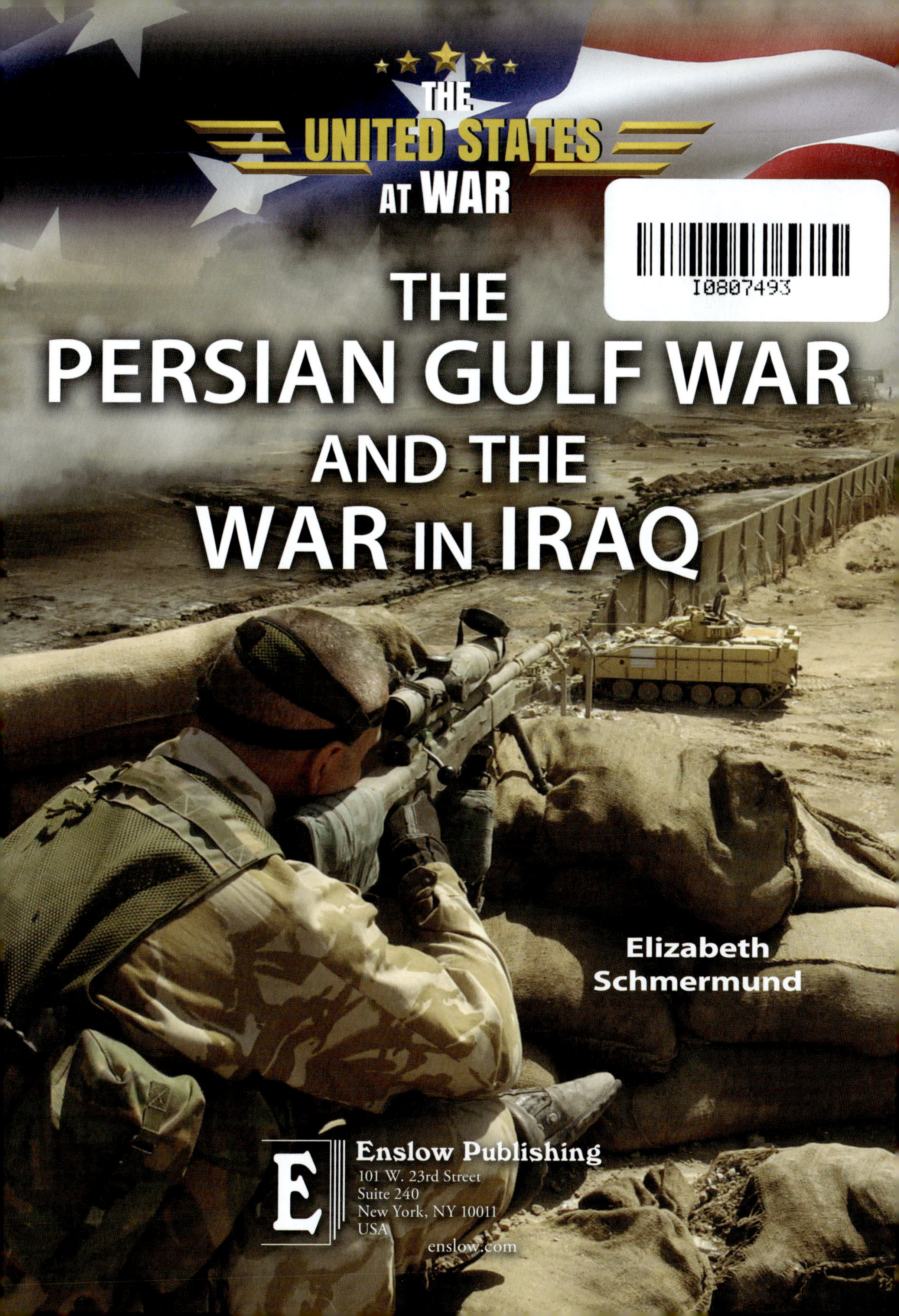

Elizabeth Schmermund

Enslow Publishing
101 W. 23rd Street
Suite 240
New York, NY 10011
USA
enslow.com

Published in 2017 by Enslow Publishing, LLC.
101 W. 23rd Street, Suite 240, New York, NY 10011

Library of Congress Cataloging-in-Publication Data

Names: Schmermund, Elizabeth, author.
Title: The Persian Gulf War and the War in Iraq / Elizabeth Schmermund.
Description: New York, NY : Enslow Publishing, 2017. | Series: The United States at war | Includes bibliographical references and index.
Identifiers: LCCN 2016004690 | ISBN 9780766076808 (library bound)
Subjects: LCSH: Iraq War, 2003-2011. | Persian Gulf War, 1991.
Classification: LCC DS79.76 .S3348 2016 | DDC 956.7044/3—dc23
LC record available at http://lccn.loc.gov/2016004690

Printed in the United States of America

To Our Readers: We have done our best to make sure all websites in this book were active and appropriate when we went to press. However, the author and the publisher have no control over and assume no liability for the material available on those websites or on any websites they may link to. Any comments or suggestions can be sent by e-mail to customerservice@enslow.com.

Photo Credits: Cover, pp. 1, Memory Stockphoto/Shutterstock.com (insignia), Sergey Kamshylin/Shutterstock.com (US flag); 67 © AP Images; pp. 4–5, 6, 70 Ramzi Haidar/AFP/Getty Images; p. 14 AFP/Getty Images; p. 16 iStock/Thinkstock; p. 20 Bassignac/Saussier/Gamma-Rapho/Getty Images; p. 22 Rusian Olinchuk/Alamy Stock Photo; p. 27 © Johnny Saunderson/Alamy Stock Photo; p. 29 Faleh Kheiber/Reuters/ Newscom; p. 34 Hugo Philpott/AFP/Getty Images; p. 37 Department of Defense photo by Staff Sgt. Dean Wagner; p. 40 © Jassim Mohammed/AP Photo; p. 42 Kaveh Kazemi/Hulton Achive/Getty Images; p. 46 Spencer Platt/Getty Images; p. 50 Doug Kanter/AFP/Getty Images; p. 53 Michael Bradley/AsiaPac/Getty Images; p. 55 U.S. Department of State/ Getty Images; p. 58 Patrick Baz/AFP/Getty Images; p. 62 Stephen Jaffe/AFP/Getty Images; pp. 64, 86 Getty Images; p. 68 Sabah Arar/AFP/Getty Images; p. 72 Mehdi Fedouach/AFP/Getty Image; p. 76 Scott Peterson/Getty Images; p. 82 Laurent Van Der/ Gamma-Rapho/Getty Images; p. 92 ADuran/Wikimedia Commons/Iraq-War-Map; p. 94 John Moore/Getty Images; p. 96 Mario Tama/Getty Images; p. 100 Muhannad Fala'ah/ Getty Images; p, 105 Universal History Archive/UIG via Getty Images.

CONTENTS

FOREWORD 4

CHAPTER 1
Early Beginnings 6

CHAPTER 2
The 100-Hour War 22

CHAPTER 3
Legacy of the Persian Gulf War .. 34

CHAPTER 4
Steps to the Iraq War 46

CHAPTER 5
Operation Iraqi Freedom 58

CHAPTER 6
The War Intensifies 76

CHAPTER 7
The Civil Conflict and the Surge . 86

CHAPTER 8
After the Withdrawal, A New Enemy 96

Chronology 112

Chapter Notes 115

Glossary 122

For More Information 124

Index 126

FOREWORD

The wars in Iraq have touched the lives of generations around the globe. Thousands of American soldiers were sent to the Persian Gulf War from 1990 to 1991, and then to the Iraq War from 2003 until 2011. These wars cost the lives of thousands of American soldiers and Kuwaitis, and hundreds of thousands of Iraqis. Despite these immense losses, there seems to be no end in sight. Extensions of these wars continue to the present day and have created a pervading sense of fear. It seems the experiences of war have crept into every household.

On September 11, 2001, as I sat in a high school history classroom in New York and watched images of planes flying into the World Trade Center on TV, the war invaded my life. Years later, I met a man whose father had fled Iraq as a young

man. He eventually became my husband, and his Iraqi family became my family. One rainy spring in 2008, members of my husband's family fled the violence of Iraq by car, winding northwest through the country of Syria. At home, we desperately awaited news of their arrival. They made it, but so many other families didn't. Today, thousands of refugees attempt this same dangerous journey. So many of their journeys end in tragedy.

We retell history in the hopes that the younger generation will not repeat our mistakes. Amid the constant cries for war, we should step back and reflect on its true cost, for us and for our children. One day I hope that I can tell my son that his grandfather's country is at peace. Until then, we will tell a story of remembrance.

1

EARLY BEGINNINGS

"DURING THE GULF WAR, I REMEMBER TWO LITTLE THIRD GRADE GIRLS SAYING TO ME—AFTER I READ THEM SOME POEMS BY WRITERS IN IRAQ—'YOU KNOW, WE NEVER THOUGHT ABOUT THERE BEING CHILDREN IN IRAQ BEFORE.' AND I THOUGHT, 'WELL THOSE POEMS DID THEIR JOB, BECAUSE NOW THEY'LL THINK ABOUT EVERYTHING A LITTLE BIT DIFFERENTLY.'"[1]

— Poet Naomi Shihab Nye

Early in the morning of March 20, 2003, bombs sliced through the air as they were dropped over Baghdad, the capital of Iraq. The people of Iraq had seen many wars, but little compared to the devastation that they saw that day. Struck by powerful missiles, buildings crumbled to the ground. People cowered in their homes and prayed that their roofs would not fall down on them. An air raid siren blared above the sounds of explosions.

American president George W. Bush had announced two days earlier that Saddam Hussein, the president of Iraq, had forty-eight hours to leave the country. If he didn't, the American military would attack. Hussein didn't listen to President Bush's warnings and, ninety minutes after the deadline passed, the American invasion of Iraq began. As the attacks continued to devastate the country, an Iraqi official spoke over the radio to his fellow countrymen. "God protect us from foreign aggressors," his voice rang out. "God give us patience. God protect our leader."[2] Saddam Hussein, fearing for his life, was nowhere to be found; he had already gone into hiding.

Many Americans and Iraqis believe that the American invasion of Iraq in 2003 was set into motion by events that began many years before. Some say it began in 1990, when Saddam Hussein annexed the small country of Kuwait. Following this action, President George H.W. Bush, President George W. Bush's father, ordered American troops into Iraq. This chain of events began the Persian Gulf War. Some people said that it had even started years before this war, when Saddam Hussein first became president of Iraq. Whenever these tensions between the United States and Iraq began, the consequences were deadly. Hundreds of thousands of Iraqis—both soldiers and civilians— and thousands of Americans were killed during the Persian Gulf War, which lasted from

1990 to 1991, and the Iraq War, which lasted from 2003 to 2011.

Iraq

Iraq is a country of arresting beauty that is home to the some of the oldest cultures in the world. It shares a border with six different countries—Turkey, Iran, Kuwait, Saudi Arabia, Jordan, and Syria, not to mention the autonomous Iraqi Kurdistan to the north—and the cultures of its many regions differ greatly.

Arab Iraqis, often living in tribes, inhabit the vast deserts that spread across Iraq's west and southwest. The Kurds, with their own culture and religion, live in the highlands to the northeast of Iraq. There, huge mountains emerge from the landscape, creating steep canyons and crags across the border with Iran. The northwestern plains of Upper Mesopotamia are where the great Assyrian Empire emerged four thousand years ago. The Assyrians of Iraq are descended from the creators of this great civilization and still speak its ancient language, called Aramaic, today.

The region between the Tigris and Euphrates Rivers that extends from northern Iraq to the southeast is known as "the cradle of civilization," or the Fertile Crescent, and contains the ruins of great ancient cities such as Babylon and Ur. In the southeast of Iraq, where the Tigris and Euphrates Rivers merge, the great Iraqi marshes once spread over thousands of miles. Although much of this marshland was drained during Saddam Hussein's reign, the marshes still play an important role in the lives of the Iraqis who live there. The Marsh Arabs, as they are known, are descended from the ancient Sumerians. They still build houses made entirely from reeds, as their ancestors did thousands of years ago, and they use boats to travel from one house to another.

Fishermen in Baghdad catch *masgouf* and cook it in open-air fire pits along the banks of the Tigris River. This is Iraq's national dish. Lamb kebabs, lamb stew with okra, and *dolma*, or meat-stuffed vegetables, are also popular dishes. Iraq is also the world's largest producer of dates. Tea is popular in Iraq, and any guest who enters an Iraqi home will be offered steaming tea and plates of delicious food.

A Complex History

The relationship between Iraq and the United States is a long and complicated one. The leaders and politicians of Iraq and the United States have been allies, or strategic partners, as well as adversaries. Before the Gulf War broke out in 1990, tensions had been increasing between these two countries for nearly thirty years. And since the Gulf War, the United States has continued its policies of military intervention in Iraq through to the present day.

Iraq's history has also been long and complex. It was part of the Ottoman Empire from the late

1700s until 1918. When the Ottoman Empire lost to Britain, France, and the United States during World War I, its land was redistributed. Iraq then became a British mandate. This means that, while Iraq had some level of freedom, its government was administered by Great Britain. The people of Iraq were not happy with this, since they had been promised that they would be allowed to govern themselves once the Ottoman Empire was broken up. Finally, in 1933, the country gained its independence and became the Kingdom of Iraq. This wasn't the end of Britain's—or, Britain's ally, the United States'—involvement in Iraq, however. During World War II, a group of men overthrew the Iraqi monarchy. A month-long war began between Britain and Iraq, with the British government succeeding in restoring power to the previous monarchy. After the British won the war, many in Iraq grew angry that a foreign nation was able to play such a large role in Iraq's government. These people thought that Iraqis should govern their own country without any outside influence. If they wanted to overthrow their own monarch, what business was it of Britain's or any other country's? Their anger simmered just below the surface for more than fifteen years.

Then, in 1958, another successful coup d'état, or attempt to overthrow the existing government, ended the Iraqi monarchy. Known as the 14 July Revolution, it brought a man named General Abd al-Karim Qasim to power. General Qasim was tall and thin, and he wore a well-groomed mustache for most of his life. His friends called him "the snake charmer." He had many goals for Iraq, including improving the educational system, establishing greater equality for women, and redistributing land to Iraq's poorer citizens.

This was the end of the Kingdom of Iraq, and the beginning of the Republic of Iraq. But although this new Iraq was called a republic, which means that the people are in control of the government, the reality was much different. General Qasim was a dictator who held complete power over the people of Iraq and did not allow anyone to go against him. Many Iraqis fled his oppressive regime following the 14 July Revolution, including many members of the Baath Party. The Baath Party was a political party that wanted to unite all Arab countries together in order to create a society based on socialism. They were at odds with General Qasim, who did not believe in pan-Arabism.

Hearing about the Iraqi revolution in the United States, the American government grew very worried. Like the British, they had interests in Iraq that they wanted to protect. General Qasim was also a communist, and the American government was afraid of the spread of communism across the Middle East. According to a US Senate report, the Central Intelligence Agency (CIA) planned to assassinate General Qasim in 1960 by giving him a poisoned handkerchief.

Some people say the handkerchief was never sent, and some say that Qasim never received it. Whatever the case, General Qasim survived that assassination attempt. But he would not survive another one, to come in February 1963.

On February 8, 1963, Baath Party members struck against Qasim and his government. They arrested or killed top-ranking officials in the Communist Party and rolled tanks through the streets of Baghdad. General Qasim sought refuge by hiding in a government building, but he was soon discovered. On February 9, 1963, he was shot and killed. Later, documents came to light that showed that the American government had known about the coup d'état before it happened. Some people claim the American government helped the Baath Party members in the uprising against General Qasim. Whatever the case, this coup brought the Baath Party to power in Iraq—a party that a young man named Saddam Hussein would later rule.

President Saddam Hussein

The Baath Party now held power in Iraq, although there were multiple changes in leadership from 1963 until 1968. Another, final coup in 1968 (called a bloodless revolution because of its lack of violence) finally brought Saddam Hussein to an important position in the government. He spent ten years as the vice president of Iraq, behind the president Ahmed Hassan Bakr. Then, when Bakr resigned from office for health reasons in 1979, Saddam Hussein stepped up to become the new president of Iraq. This marked a new era in Iraq's history.

Saddam Hussein was no stranger to politics when he became vice president in 1968. He had joined the Baath party when he was just twenty years old because his uncle was a supporter. The pan-Arab Baath Party was originally a socialist party that wanted to create a large alliance between Arab countries; they grew angry at the Communist Party, headed by Qasim, when it refused to join such an alliance. When the Baath Party attempted to assassinate Qasim in 1959, Hussein played a major role in the operation. In fact, he was accused of ruining it. Another would-be assassin later accused Hussein of firing too quickly on the car that carried General Qasim through the streets of Baghdad, alerting him to the danger. The

This photo of young Saddam Hussein was taken in 1960, when he was a leader of the Baath party.

assassination attempt failed, and Hussein was forced to flee to neighboring Syria. He stayed in Syria, and then in Egypt, until the successful coup of 1963 made it safe for him to return.

As the president of Iraq, Saddam Hussein took strong measures to guard his power. His secret police imprisoned, tortured, and killed anyone who spoke out against him or his government. Later on, he committed mass genocide against the Kurdish people, an ethnic group within Iraq who wanted their own government. This was called the al-Anfal Campaign. From 1986 to 1989, Hussein's government exterminated up to one hundred thousand innocent people in this genocidal campaign. He dropped chemical weapons on villages and tortured, "disappeared," and killed military-age Kurdish men and boys.

Saddam Hussein seemed to enjoy holding such power over the life and death of his people. He erected statues of himself around the country, made his books required reading in schools, and plastered his image everywhere. He consolidated his power until he was the absolute ruler over his country, and then used this power to control all of the different religious and ethnic groups within Iraq. Few people spoke out against Saddam Hussein's reign. If they did, they were usually tortured and killed. Only a few were lucky enough to flee their country. But, perhaps worst of all, Hussein would continue to lead his country and his people into war after war.

Iraq is the blue country in the center here. It has uneasy relations with many of its neighbors, especially Iran (yellow).

The Iran-Iraq War

In September 1980, just shortly after Saddam Hussein became president, Iraq entered into the Iran-Iraq War. The two neighboring countries have historically had a troubled history because of border disputes. Iran and Iraq share a border and neither country can agree on exactly where each country begins and ends. After the 1979 Iranian Revolution, Hussein viewed the new religious government in Iran as a threat to his own secular government. He invaded Iran on September 22 with air strikes and simultaneous ground strikes. This war would last eight years and resulted in more than five hundred thousand casualties.[3] The losses were all for nothing, unfortunately, as neither side won the war.

During the eight years of the Iran-Iraq War, the United States aided Iraq by providing Saddam Hussein with weapons and military intelligence. The two countries had generally good diplomatic relations at this time. This began to change, however, when Hussein discovered that the United States had also secretly been providing Iran with weapons during several years of the war. Hussein remained suspicious of the United States, although both countries continued to build their relationship as allies.

The Persian Gulf War

Though the Iran-Iraq War was over, the people of Iraq, a country that had experienced an almost continuous succession of wars, would not experience peace for long. When the British recognized the Kingdom of Iraq in 1922, they had split areas of land that had once been ruled together under the Ottoman Empire. This created the country of Kuwait from land that many Iraqis believed should belong to Iraq. This division of land also created another problem for Iraq and, later, for Saddam Hussein: the newly drawn borders of Iraq gave the country little access to water. This was a strategic problem for both trade and military reasons. Saddam Hussein believed that Kuwait belonged to Iraq and that the land had been stolen from his country. In 1990, Saddam Hussein accused Kuwait of drilling for oil on land on the border of Iraq and Kuwait. He claimed that Kuwait was profiting off land that belonged to Iraq. This accusation was one more step on the steady march to the Persian Gulf War.

Some people view the Persian Gulf War as an extension of the Iran-Iraq War. After this eight-year war, Iraq was in debt, and asked the government of Kuwait to forgive its debts to them. When Kuwait refused, tensions increased between the two countries, leading Hussein to claim that he would take back land that rightfully belonged to Iraq. In addition to this, Hussein accused Kuwait of producing more oil than it was allowed to produce. This overproduction made oil prices go down, which hurt Iraq's economy because they were forced to sell their own oil for less money than they otherwise would. At the beginning of July 1990, Saddam Hussein declared that if Kuwait did not respect Iraq's wishes, it would take action.

The United States, which had recently been enjoying warmer relations with Iraq, grew concerned with Hussein's threats. It sent military planes and ships to the Persian Gulf as a warning to Iraq that it should not take any action against Kuwait. Then the American ambassador to Iraq, a woman named April Glaspie, met with Saddam Hussein on July 25.[4] Hussein expressed his anger that the United States, with whom he was allied, would not support his actions. Hussein threatened to send a message directly to American president George H.W. Bush to let him know how he felt. In the end, though he was disappointed that the United States would not take his side, he agreed to continue negotiating with the Kuwaiti government. The United States knew that there continued to be political tension due to this conflict between Iraq and Kuwait, but the American government did not think that Saddam Hussein would begin an outright war against Kuwait at this time.

They were wrong. Early in the morning on August 2, 1990, Iraq bombed Kuwait City, the capital of Kuwait. Iraqi troops stormed through the small country, easily entering into the capital city. Despite months of threats, the Kuwaitis were shocked. Small battles continued throughout the

This is the Kuwait City airport after the bombs were dropped there by Iraq.

day in the deserts stretching along the Iraqi border and along the cosmopolitan and wealthy coast of Kuwait. The heaviest fighting amongst Iraqi and Kuwaiti soldiers occurred in front of Kuwait's royal palace. Sheikh Sabah, the ruler of Kuwait, fled to Saudi Arabia, but his brother remained behind to defend Dasman Palace and was killed.[5] Soon, Iraqi soldiers had taken over the airwaves, declaring Kuwait's government had changed hands.

This attack left the world stunned. Within hours of Iraq's surprise attack on Kuwait, the United Nations, with a request made by both the United States and Kuwait, condemned Hussein's actions and soon placed economic sanctions on Iraq. Economic sanctions are penalties that a group of countries places on another country that has gone against international rules and agreements; this meant that certain countries would not trade with Iraq, which would hurt the country economically.

Unfortunately, for the people of Iraq, this would begin a new era of continued military struggle and political instability. Saddam Hussein's fear of losing power led to his attack on Iran. His invasion of Kuwait grew from the drawn-out war with Iran and would contribute to the Persian Gulf War. Many years later, political and military historians would say that the Persian Gulf War would lead to the Iraq War of 2003. This unending series of wars hurt nobody more than the Iraqi civilians who lived through years of bombings and attacks. Year after year, Iraqi civilians, as well as civilians in Iran and Kuwait, would have to deal with violence, insecurity, economic difficulty, and the pain and grief of sending their fathers and sons off to war. Though Hussein has not been president of Iraq since 2003, Saddam Hussein's decisions continue to spell disaster for the people of Iraq.

2 THE 100-HOUR WAR

"A LINE HAS BEEN DRAWN IN THE SAND… WITHDRAW FROM KUWAIT UNCONDITIONALLY AND IMMEDIATELY, OR FACE THE TERRIBLE CONSEQUENCES."

— President George H.W. Bush[1]

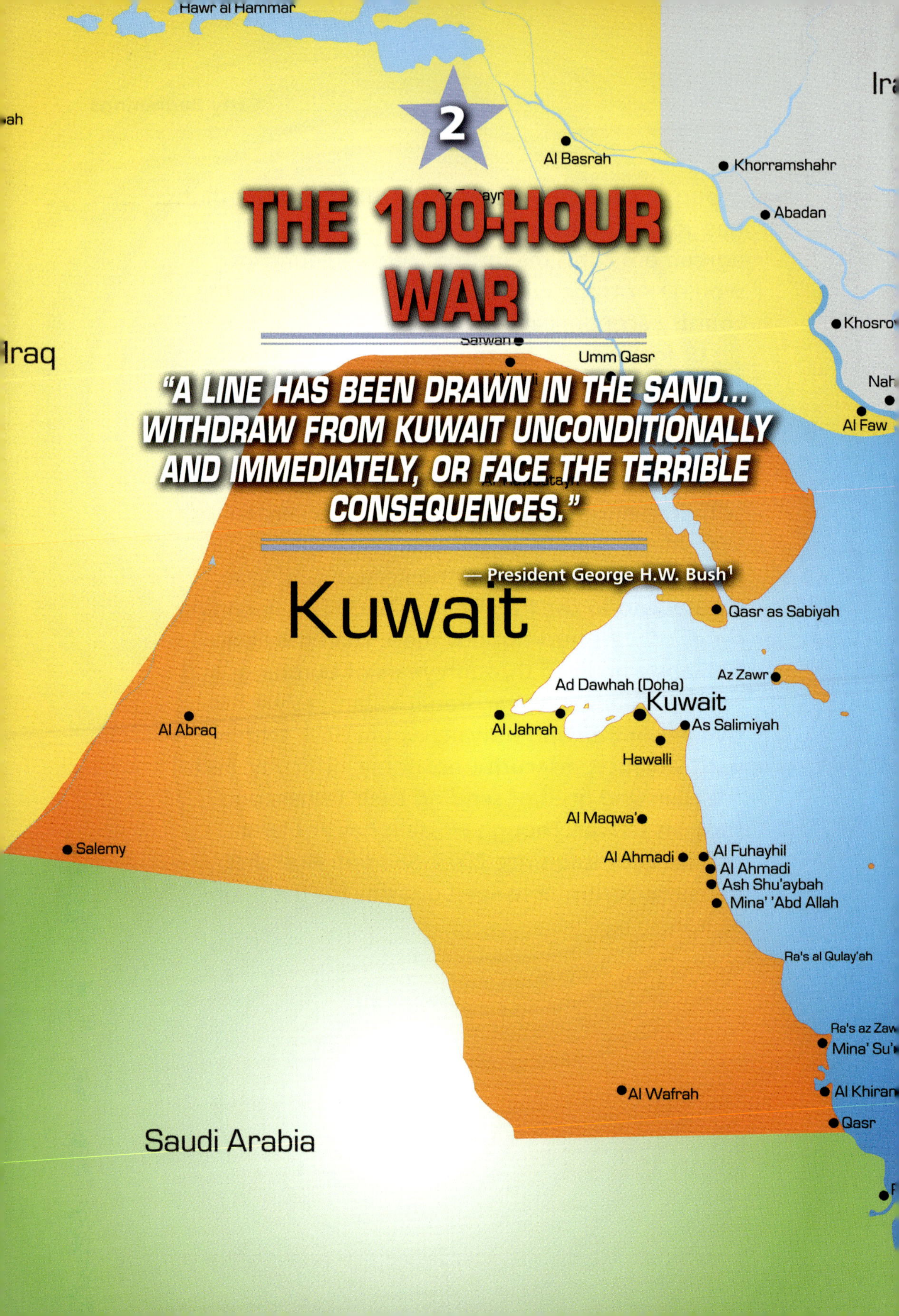

When Iraq attacked Kuwait on August 2, 1990, the international community scrambled to figure out how to address this act of war. At first, Saddam Hussein planned to set up a new government in Kuwait with pro-Iraqi Kuwaitis. He deposed the emir, or ruler, of Kuwait and confiscated all of the royal family's money on August 3. The next day, the United Nations issued a formal order for Iraq to withdraw from Kuwait. Economic sanctions began on August 6.

Saddam Hussein, however, ignored these pleas from the international community. On August 8, he formally annexed Kuwait, declaring it a territory of Iraq, and abandoned his original plan to set up a pro-Iraqi government made up of Kuwaitis. This action showed that Hussein did not plan to stop military action or withdraw from Kuwait. By annexing Kuwait, Saddam Hussein challenged other nations, including the United States, to get involved militarily.

President George H.W. Bush struggled to determine what action American forces should take, especially since American-Iraqi relations had recently improved. However, as a close ally of Saudi Arabia, a country that felt threatened by Iraq's actions in the Middle East, Bush felt that the United States would likely need to intervene. Publicly, President Bush stated that Saddam Hussein's invasion of Kuwait would not be accepted. Privately, he met with European allies and tried to figure out a solution that would get Iraq out of Kuwait without too much bloodshed. Meanwhile, the king of Saudi Arabia met with the American Secretary of Defense, Dick Cheney, and requested US military assistance. The king feared that if Hussein had invaded oil-rich Kuwait, there was not much to stop him from invading Saudi Arabia as well, which was another country with access to a lot of oil.

In addition to Saudi Arabia's request for military aid, Israel sent a delegation to

Washington, DC, to express their fear of the likelihood that Hussein would attack Israel following his attack on Kuwait. Partly in response to the pressure from these allies, the United States sent Air Force fighter jets into Kuwait. At first they did not attack. These fighter jets simply remained there as a warning to Hussein as negotiations began between the United States and Iraq. During talks, Saddam Hussein said that he would withdraw from half of Kuwait if he would be allowed to occupy the other half. President Bush refused this request and plans for a ground invasion to free Kuwait from the Iraqi military began. General Norman Schwarzkopf would lead the American troops.

Speaking in front of the United States Congress, President Bush outlined his goals for any military action they might take against Iraq's invasion of Kuwait:

> Iraq must withdraw from Kuwait completely, immediately and without condition. Kuwait's legitimate government must be restored. The security and stability of the Persian Gulf must be assured. And American citizens abroad must be protected. Out of these troubled times, our fifth objective—a new world order—can emerge: a new era—freer from the threat of terror, stronger in the pursuit of justice, and more secure in the quest for peace.[2]

All Means Necessary

On November 29, the UN Security Council authorized the use of "all means necessary" to remove Iraqi forces from Kuwait. This meant that the United States and any allies would have permission to use military strikes against Iraq. In mid-January, the American Congress authorized the use of force to remove Iraqi forces from Kuwait. This was the permission that was needed for President Bush to begin a military campaign against Iraq if Saddam Hussein ignored the final deadline to remove his troops from the neighboring country. On January 15, the United Nations' deadline for Iraqi withdrawal from Kuwait came and went. Hussein made no move to withdraw. On January 17, the American and allied forces began their attacks.

The United States allied with Kuwait, Great Britain, Saudi Arabia, France, Italy, Canada, Egypt and several other countries to fight against Iraq's actions in Kuwait. Thirty-four countries in all made up the allied coalition. Together, they began air strikes, which were later followed with troops on the ground. The United States named this Operation Desert Storm. They planned first to destroy Iraq's Air Force and antiaircraft facilities that housed missiles that could shoot down American and allied planes. Then they would target Iraqi command facilities and various military targets throughout both Iraq and Kuwait.

American soldiers march toward Checkpoint Charlie on the Basra Road in Iraq, in 1991. This was the southernmost point of American occupation at this point in the war.

Beginning early on the morning of January 17, allied forces conducted more than 4,000 bombing runs, a number that would reach 110,000 by the end of the war.[3] The American Air Force continued to drop bombs across Iraq and Kuwait, devastating Iraqi infrastructure and military facilities, for three long weeks.

On February 15, Iraq's government stated that the Iraqi military would leave Kuwait. It seemed as if the allied air strikes had been successful. There were celebrations in the streets of Baghdad and Kuwait, showing how unpopular the war was even with Iraqis. But Saddam Hussein followed up this announcement with conditions that were unacceptable to the international community. Iraqi troops did not withdraw from Kuwait after all, and the air war kept raging.

Operation Desert Sabre

The allied coalition knew that for a complete victory, they would need to send in ground troops. On February 24, 1991, the first allied troops began their ground assault in what became known as Operation Desert Sabre. Altogether, the allied coalition consisted of 670,000 troops. Of this, the great majority—425,000 in all—of these troops were from the United States.[4] One day before the ground attacks were to begin, American Special Forces teams entered into Iraq secretly. Then, other group's troops pushed west into Kuwait from Saudi Arabia on the following day. At the same time, different troops drove into Iraq and captured Iraq's reserve soldiers and any retreating troops. It became obvious very quickly that Iraq could not win the war. In fact, it seemed as if Saddam Hussein knew this, too. The Iraqi Air Force didn't fight back much against allied attacks; instead, Iraqi pilots would fly across the Iraq border into Iran, making emergency landings in hidden areas. It seemed that Saddam Hussein's plan was to protect Iraqi aircrafts at all costs, to use after the war.

The Cost of the War

This doesn't mean that everything went smoothly; wars never do. Throughout February, concern

Amir Adnan was the only survivor of the Amiriyah shelter bombing. His seven-member family was among those killed in the attack.

began to grow about the number of civilian casualties in Iraq. Bombs that landed near Baghdad did not only destroy strategic targets, such as military facilities, they also destroyed many civilian homes. On February 13, allied bombs hit the Amiriyah air raid shelter in Baghdad. Allied forces stated that their intelligence reports showed that it was a military base. However, hundreds of civilians were inside, almost entirely women and children seeking safety from the bombs that were falling around them. They assumed that a shelter would not be targeted, but they were wrong. At least 408 innocent civilians were killed when the shelter was hit.[5] Many countries criticized the United States for these civilian deaths.

On February 25, a missile hit barracks where American soldiers were staying in Saudi Arabia, killing 28 Americans, wounding 98, and seriously injuring 110.[6] That same day millions of tons of oil were dumped into the Persian Gulf, causing the largest oil slick in history. Iraqi soldiers dumped the oil, hoping to stop a potential landing on the site by US forces and to make it hard for them to get any oil. The slick extended 101 miles (162 km) and was five inches (12.7 cm) thick in some areas.[7] Thousands of sea birds and marine life were killed due to the harmful effects of the oil. Scientists stated that it would take decades to recover from the massive environmental damage caused by this oil spill.

When ground troops began their assault, air strikes began to slow. Threatened by the approaching allied troops, Iraqi forces began to burn Kuwait's oil fields. Hussein wanted to seek revenge on the Kuwaiti royal family for drilling on what he considered to be Iraqi land, as well as for overproducing oil. There was also a strategic reason for burning Kuwaiti oil. The fires would create enough smoke to hide Iraqi forces, making it harder for the Americans and their allies to target them. Although these fires had been set earlier in the war as well, they began to occur much more frequently when the allied ground troops were sent in. Approximately 700 oil wells (out of Kuwait's 1000) were set on fire, causing huge environmental damage. According to scientists, smoke from the fires absorbed up to 80 percent of the sun's rays, leaving the areas around them dark and cold even during the day.[8]

The War Comes to an End

After the ground attack, Saddam Hussein spoke to the Iraqi people over the radio and claimed that Iraq would win the war. He was trying to bolster support for a cause that was already lost. Despite his posturing, on the battlefields, Iraqi soldiers placed their weapons down on the ground and began to flee. Many surrendered. They felt that they could not win the war and hoped they would be allowed to return home safely to their families if they surrendered to the American forces.

On February 26, after only two days of fighting, allied forces gained control of Kuwait City. The next day, on February 27, Saddam Hussein called for a cease-fire, which President Bush rejected. He did not trust that Hussein would keep his word. The ground attack continued, but it would last only one more day. Fleeing Iraqi soldiers were being attacked and killed by air raids. People around the world called for President Bush to end the war and the unnecessary killings. On February 28, only one hundred hours after the ground assault began, President Bush called for a cease-fire. He stated that the allies had won and that there was no point continuing the war. Everyone, including the government and people of Iraq, agreed.

Iraq surrendered and officially brought the Persian Gulf War to an end on March 3, 1991, when General Schwarzkopf met with Iraqi commanders in southern Iraq. Allied forces surrounded the table where they met, with tanks draped in American flags. On April 3, the UN Security Council passed a resolution that formally brought the Persian Gulf War to an end. This resolution established measures that Iraq would need to follow to avoid sanctions or other repercussions. Some of these measures included respecting the boundary between Kuwait and Iraq, destroying all of its chemical and biological weapons, returning prisoners of war, and paying for all damages to Kuwait. The resolution ended like this: "The Security Council shall determine the existence of any threat to the peace...or act of aggression...and decide what measures shall be taken...to maintain or restore international peace and security."[9] This one sentence, allowing the UN Security Council to use any means necessary to prevent Iraq's further aggressions, would be invoked again in the lead-up to the 2003 US-led invasion of Iraq.

3

LEGACY OF THE GULF WAR

"THE NUMBER OF PEOPLE KILLED BY THE SANCTIONS IN IRAQ IS GREATER THAN THE TOTAL NUMBER OF PEOPLE KILLED BY ALL WEAPONS OF MASS DESTRUCTION IN ALL OF HISTORY"

— John and Karl Mueller[1]

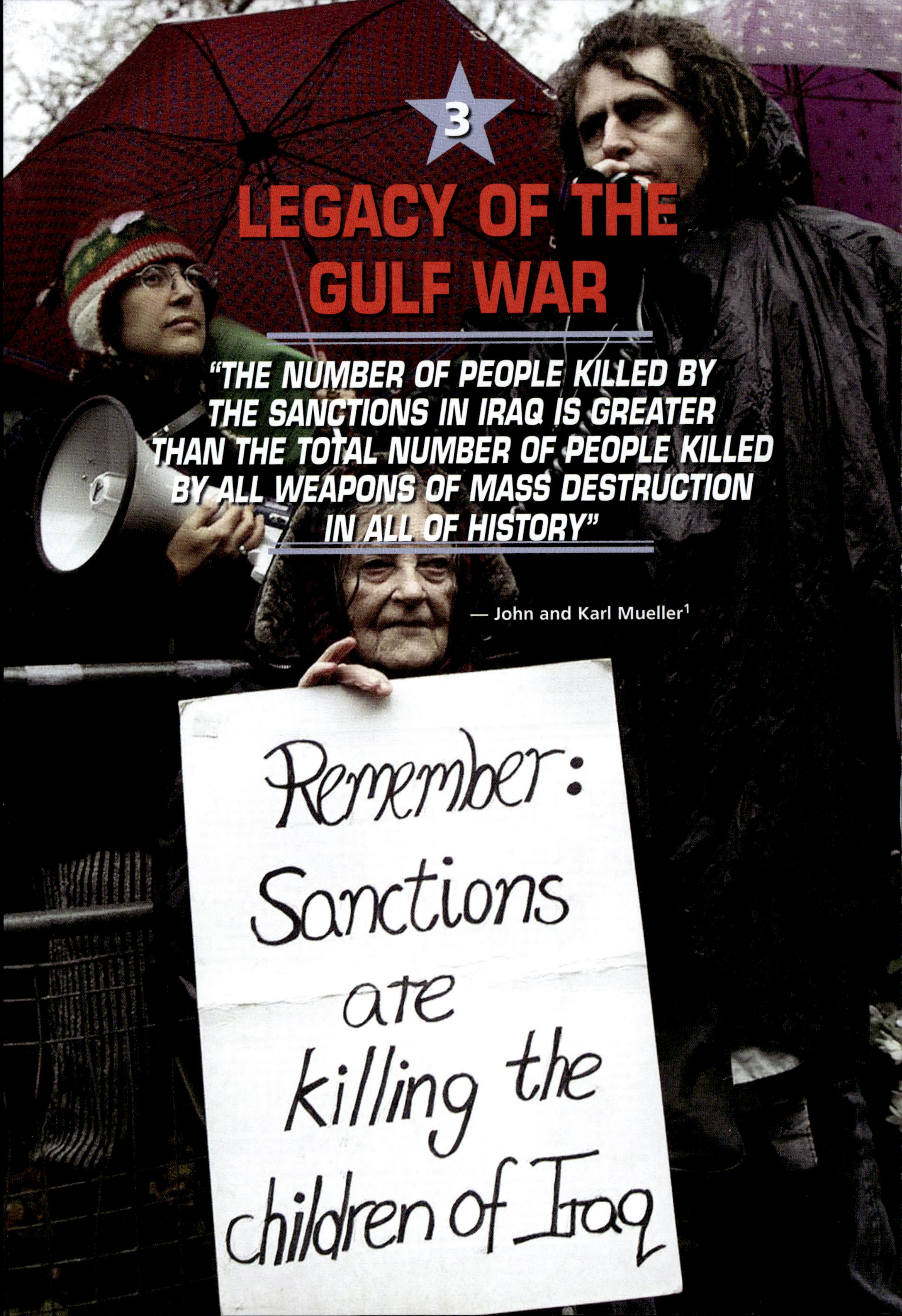

Although the Gulf War lasted a very short time, it caused great devastation. Over one thousand Kuwaiti citizens were killed and six hundred went missing during the period of Iraq's invasion, from August 1990 until allied forces liberated Kuwait City on February 26, 1991. Later, hundreds of mass graves would be discovered across the vast deserts of Kuwait.

Loss of Life

Civilians, in particular, were the victims of this war. During the early stages of the war, allied forces bombed Iraq heavily, causing many casualties among people who were not military personnel. According to some figures, over 3,500 Iraqi civilians were killed from the allied bombings.[2] Other figures have shown that over 70,000 Iraqi civilians died from war-related damage to medical facilities and supplies, water facilities, and the power grid.[3] During and immediately after the war, no official figures were taken, and there has been no consensus as to the exact numbers of the dead. However, we do know that many civilians were killed or wounded, and that many others had to deal with a lack of food and clean water, as well as a shortage of medical supplies. This was the greatest harm to human life: bombs killed many people, but damage done to key infrastructure and a shortage of food, water, and medical supplies killed many more over a longer period of time.

When Iraqi soldiers heard that allied ground troops were approaching Kuwait City, they burned and looted homes and businesses, and tortured and abused Kuwaiti men and women. It seemed they did this in a panic, trying to cause the most amount of damage before they were captured or forced to retreat. Iraqi forces captured over six hundred Kuwaiti soldiers, who were never to be heard from again and presumably were killed.

Thousands of people were killed and many Iraqi tanks and trucks were destroyed by the United States and their allies during the Gulf War.

Once the allied forces arrived, the killings only intensified. Tony Clifton, an American journalist reporting for *Newsweek*, described the scene when American forces targeted the fleeing Iraqis: "At its peak, the scene looked like something out of a medieval artist's vision of hell, a great backdrop of leaping flames against which we could see the tiny figures of men frantically trying to escape the fire."[4] The Iraq government did not disclose the exact number of casualties it suffered, but a US Air Force study estimated that more than 20,000 were killed.[5] Some say that this estimate is too low and judge the real number of Iraqi combatant deaths to be around 35,000. Over 70,000 Iraqi soldiers were wounded.[6]

Allied coalition forces suffered far fewer losses than the Iraqis, although any loss of life is devastating. The coalition lost 358 troops in total—of these, 114 were American. Forty-four American soldiers were killed mistakenly by friendly fire. In total, 776 coalition troops were wounded during the war, including 458 Americans.[7]

Economic Losses

The tragic consequences of the Persian Gulf War would continue long after the fighting stopped. The US Congress calculated the cost of the war to the United States at $61.1 billion.[8] Iraq's economy suffered enormous losses due to damage and lost income sustained during the war. Gulf War debts for Iraq totaled $110 billion, on top of the debt left over from the Iran-Iraq War, which totaled $300 billion.[9] Iraq would never recover these losses under Saddam Hussein.

Sanctions

As part of the cease-fire agreement, Saddam Hussein agreed to accept certain conditions. He promised to respect the disputed border between Iraq and Kuwait, which would be guarded by UN forces. He also agreed to destroy or remove all chemical and biological weapons and ballistic missiles. Until these weapons were destroyed, the United Nations imposed economic sanctions against Iraq.

In the late 1980s, Saddam Hussein had used these weapons during the Iran-Iraq War. He also employed them against some of his own people, an ethnic minority in the north of Iraq called the Kurds, during the al-Anfal Campaign. Recently, studies have shown that chemical weapons in military facilities bombed by coalition forces escaped into the air. Coalition forces breathed in these chemical weapons and got very sick. These weapons had not been developed during the Persian Gulf War, but were left over from the Iran-Iraq War.

For many years, Iraq was allowed to import food into the country only on a case-by-case basis. This meant that food imports were very limited, and many Iraqis did not have enough to eat. In

Women wait in line as their food rations are measured out. The rations had been increased just before this photo was taken as part of the "Oil for Food" program.

late 1997, the United Nations allowed Iraq to sell oil in exchange for food. This wasn't enough to reverse the damage already done on the Iraq population. Other sanctions, such as limits on importing medical supplies, would only be lifted after all chemical and biological weapons and ballistic missiles were removed. In addition, Iraq would have to pay for all the damages it caused during the war. This was a big problem for Iraq, which already had a lot of debt.

These sanctions against Iraq would last until 2003, although some of them continue to the present day. During this time, almost all trade in Iraq was banned or severely limited. This meant that, although Iraq continued to go further into debt, the government had no way to pay it off.

Effects of Sanctions

While these sanctions did destroy Iraq's military and weapons program, it also caused grave problems for Iraqi citizens. After the sanctions, Hussein started a rationing program to give free food to the 60 percent of Iraqi citizens who needed it following the destruction of their land, the elimination of jobs, and the loss of men who earned money for their families. However, due to a shortage in money and food, the limit was one thousand calories per person per day—not enough calories to prevent malnutrition. Approximately half of all Iraqi children under five years old were malnourished, according to a UNICEF study conducted in 2000.[10] Literacy rates plummeted, unemployment skyrocketed, and infant mortality increased. The absence of clean water and medical supplies caused disease and death. According to UN Humanitarian Coordinator Denis Halliday, 239,000 children aged five and under died from 1990 to 1998 due to these sanctions.[11] Some estimates put child mortality due to the sanctions against Iraq at 500,000. Halliday ended up resigning in protest of the sanctions, calling their effects a human tragedy.

Hussein crushed a Kurdish revolt following the Gulf War, forcing thousands of Kurds to flee Iraq.

It was in response to the international outcry against these sanctions that the United Nations began the "Oil for Food" program in 1997. As mentioned above, this program allowed Iraq to trade oil for food in order to decrease the effects of the sanctions on the Iraqi population. However, many considered that this did not do enough to help the Iraqi people. Others claimed that officials were corrupt and that Iraqi civilians did not get the food they were promised.

Fighting for Recognition

After the Gulf War, in addition to these humanitarian crises, there was political upheaval in Iraq. Ethnic and religious minorities like the Kurds in the north demanded their rights and fought against Hussein's government. They hoped that the Iraqi government was weakened enough that they would win. This was not the case, however, and they were brutally crushed. Soon, hundreds of thousands of Kurds escaped Iraq to other neighboring countries. Following continued fighting, Saddam Hussein agreed to grant autonomy to the Kurds. Iraqi Kurdistan was granted self-rule in 1991. This means that it was allowed to elect its own government following the withdrawal of Iraqi troops from the region.

Shia Muslims also demanded recognition from Saddam Hussein's regime. The Shia make up 65 percent of the population of Iraq and live mostly in the southern region of the country.[12] Shia Islam is said to have started in Iraq. The country is also home to major Shia pilgrimage sites, where hundreds of thousands of Shia Muslims travel every year to pay respect to their imams, or leaders of the Shia Muslim community who are believed to be the rightful successors to the Prophet Muhammad. Before Saddam Hussein and the Baath Party came to power in the 1960s, Shia politicians held some power in the government of Iraq. Soon, however, Shia Muslims were excluded from the political system. By 1968, Shias made up less than 6 percent of the Baath Party.[13] This led many Shia Muslims to feel that they were being left out of the political process. They felt angry. Soon, there were riots in the south of Iraq. These demands grew louder during and after the war, when Iraq's Shia population thought they would have more of a voice. Each time, however, Saddam Hussein's regime brutally crushed these political protests and demands for representation. Shias were killed in riots, and important leaders in the Shia community were imprisoned, tortured, and executed.

Operation Desert Fox

Hussein's choice to invade Kuwait brought irreversible damage to Iraq and to Iraqi citizens. For a people who had lived through generations of war, their situations seemed to only be getting worse. Following the Gulf War, the United Nations destroyed much of Iraq's chemical, biological, and nuclear weapons. Sometimes Saddam Hussein would cooperate with UN weapons inspectors, and sometimes he would not. However, beginning in 1998, Saddam Hussein refused to allow UN inspectors into Iraq. This led to Operation Desert Fox, a four-day bombing campaign led by the American and British military against Iraqi targets. Tensions flared, and many Arab nations criticized the United States and Great Britain for their actions. Iraqi and American relations continued to weaken. Hussein resented the United States for its airstrikes and UN sanctions, while the United States wanted to force Hussein into complying with weapons inspections. All of this created the perfect storm for increased political tension and eventually led to the Iraq War of 2003.

Following the Gulf War, journalist Tony Clifton expressed the devastation that he experienced and his disappointment at the continued humanitarian crisis in Iraq. He stated: "I'm opposed to war. There are no winners … War is no longer limited to the combatants but threatens all of humankind … It's a shame that [the Persian Gulf War] had to occur. It's a shame that a great number of innocents—and I mean military and civilians on both sides—have to bear the cost of the tragedy."[14]

The Persian Gulf War lasted only one hundred hours, and yet the devastation that it caused has lasted to this day.

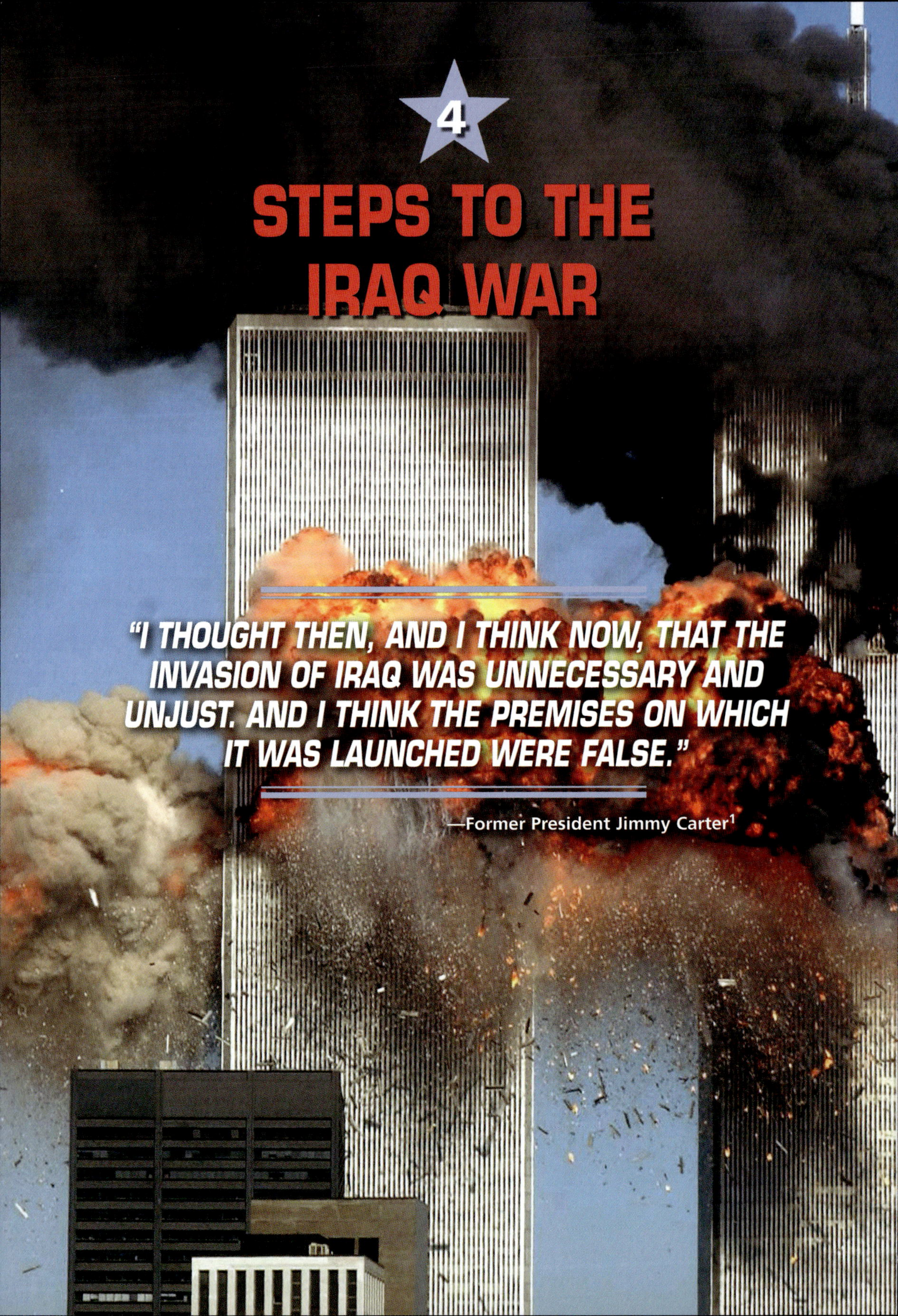

4

STEPS TO THE IRAQ WAR

"I THOUGHT THEN, AND I THINK NOW, THAT THE INVASION OF IRAQ WAS UNNECESSARY AND UNJUST. AND I THINK THE PREMISES ON WHICH IT WAS LAUNCHED WERE FALSE."

—Former President Jimmy Carter[1]

Tensions Before the War

For most of the 1990s, almost all countries except for the United States eased sanctions against Iraq. In 1994, President Clinton ordered American troops to Kuwait, fearful that Iraqi troops were poised to attack the border. Hussein withdrew his troops.

Tensions increased again when Saddam Hussein didn't allow UN weapons inspectors into Iraq. From 1997 to 2001, Iraq and the United States confronted one another again and again.

Hussein continued his refusal to allow these inspectors to enter his country. In 1998, President Clinton, who had become president after George H.W. Bush, authorized Operation Desert Fox, the code name for limited bombardments on Baghdad. They hoped the bombings would help to convince Saddam Hussein to stick to the United Nation's agreements.

In addition to this, the United States, Great Britain, and France instituted no-fly zones in Iraq following the Persian Gulf War in 1991. This meant that Iraqi aircraft could not fly over large areas of land in northern and southern Iraq. It was set up to protect the Kurds in the north and the Shias in the south against Saddam Hussein, who continued to persecute these repressed groups. In 1998, Hussein stated that the Iraqi military would shoot down any allied aircraft that flew over Iraq. However, he never actually made good on those threats. These no-fly zones continued, as did Hussein's threats against any US military aircraft flying in these areas.

When George W. Bush became president of the United States of America in January 2001, eight months before the attack on the World Trade Centers, members of his administration spent many hours deliberating over what should be done with Saddam Hussein. Some members of Bush's cabinet of advisors were extremely interested in protecting American interests abroad, especially as related to oil in the Middle

East. They suggested that Saddam Hussein should be deposed by force in order to protect the United States in case that Iraq had weapons of mass destruction. This, however, did not come to pass until nearly two years after the September 11 terror attacks.

The World Trade Center Attacks

When the first plane hit the World Trade Center's North Tower at 8:46 a.m. on September 11, 2001, the lives of people around the globe changed forever. Airplanes hijacked by nineteen Al Qaeda terrorists flew into the north and south towers of the World Trade Centers in New York and the Pentagon in Washington, DC. The fourth plane crashed into a field in Shanksville, Pennsylvania, after passengers fought against their hijackers and the plane was purposefully brought down. Nearly three thousand people were killed that day in the attacks.[2] Al Qaeda, an Islamist group led by a man named Osama bin Laden, had planned the attack against the United States for years. Nineteen hijackers—most of them from Saudi Arabia, a US ally—had carried out the plan. These attacks shook America to its core—no one had expected an attack from foreign terrorists on American soil.

Directly following the attacks on the World Trade Center, the United States declared war against the Taliban in Afghanistan. The Taliban is an Islamist political movement that had aided Al

The attacks on the World Trade Center were a devastating blow to Americans and spurred us into a lengthy war.

Qaeda in planning the attacks. But the Bush administration was also busy gathering information to justify another war in Iraq. The American government accused Saddam Hussein of harboring weapons of mass destruction (WMDs) and of aiding Al Qaeda terrorists in the attacks against the United States of America. In 2002, allied forces began a bombardment of Iraqi military facilities inside the no-fly zones in preparation for war.

Preparations for War

In October 2002, the United States Senate voted to authorize the use of the US military in Iraq. This meant that President Bush had permission from Congress to go to war with Iraq. Some senators before the vote had been told that the US military had gathered evidence that Iraq had WMDs and was possibly planning an attack on the United States with these weapons. President Bush signed a document on October 16, 2003, stating that the US military aimed to depose Saddam Hussein and replace the dictator with a democratically elected leader. In February 2003, Secretary of Defense Colin Powell presented evidence to the United Nations that Iraq was building WMDs that could reach the United States. A lot of people questioned this evidence. Later on, after the war had already begun, it was discovered that this evidence was false.[3]

President Bush began to meet with the prime minister of England, Tony Blair, at the beginning of 2003. At this point, the United States already had a military action plan. England agreed to act as an ally of the United States. The leaders of the two countries made a deal to support each other, whether or not WMDs were actually found in Iraq. They called themselves the "coalition of the willing." Altogether, forty countries joined the United States in this coalition. But only three countries, in addition to the United States, provided ground troops: Australia, Great Britain, and Poland.

Protests and Criticisms

Not everyone wanted to be in the coalition of the willing. The president of France, Jacques Chirac, refused to get involved in any military action. He declared that war should only be the last resort. Many other countries agreed with France that the United States should not strike Iraq. Even former President Bill Clinton stated that he thought military action would be a mistake. He said, "I don't care how precise your bombs and weapons are, when you set them off, innocent people will die."[4] The Bush administration moved forward with their plans anyway.

Around the world people came together to march peacefully against another US war with Iraq. From January to April of 2003, it is said that thirty-six million people protested against the war. Polls in Europe at this time showed that no more than 11 percent of Europeans believed that Americans should unilaterally carry out a war against the Hussein regime.[5] One of the main reasons against an American war in Iraq was the fact that Iraq had not carried out an attack against the United States. If the United States declared a war against Iraq, then this would be a preemptive strike, or a strike against an enemy before the enemy's attack. On February 15, 2003, coordinated antiwar protests occurred across the globe. Three million people marched in Rome, while 1.5 million people marched in Madrid.[6] Some people have described these protests as the largest antiwar movement in human history.

Beginning in 2001, Vice President Dick Cheney claimed that Iraq had financed and harbored members of Al Qaeda. However, in 2002, the CIA

Protestors in New Zealand carry a banner and signs saying, "Stop the War on Iraq.."

issued a report stating that there was no “credible intelligence reporting” of any operational relationship between Iraqi governmental officials and the Al Qaeda terrorist group. This conclusion was due, in part, to the general antipathy and distrust between Saddam Hussein and Osama bin Laden, two powerful figures who had very different goals in mind. Hussein was a secular, although brutal, ruler, while bin Laden was a religious fundamentalist who believed that a conservative interpretation of the Koran should be the basis for governmental law. To many activists in the United States and abroad, this meant that the United States was declaring war on a country that, while operated by a dictator with a dismal human rights record, had not actually attacked or planned to attack the United States. Many high-ranking political and military personnel, including members of the joint chiefs of staff, who advise the Department of Defense, Senators Edward Kennedy and Russ Feingold, and former presidential candidate Howard Dean, publicly decried the preemptive attack against Iraq.

Weapons of Mass Destruction

The United States' decision to go to war with Iraq hinged on the belief that the Hussein regime had developed WMDs. After Hussein's chemical attacks on the Kurdish people during his Al-Anfal Campaign in the late 1980s, UN weapons inspectors forced Iraq to disarm all of their chemical and biological weapons. Then, following the Persian Gulf War, Hussein was made to destroy any remaining chemical weapons. By 1999, UN inspectors stated that 90 to 95 percent of Iraqi weapons of mass destruction had been destroyed.[7] Although UN inspectors carried out this investigation, some people doubted the truth of their report due to Hussein's unwillingness to participate. United Nations' inspectors left Iraq in 1998; whether they were forced out or they had decided that no more action was necessary is still debated, and some people questioned if Saddam Hussein had been able to redevelop WMDs in the years between 1998 and 2003. In 2001, Hussein denied accusations that he had developed more weapons, stating that Iraq was not actively seeking to accumulate weapons of mass

According to the US State Department, this photo was proof that Iraq was making and moving chemical weapons and other WMDs.

destruction but that the country would always seek to defend itself against attack by other nations.

The accusation that Iraq possessed WMDs came from George W. Bush and high-placed members of his administration, including Vice President Dick Cheney, Secretary of Defense Donald Rumsfeld, and Secretaries of State Colin Powell and Condoleezza Rice. There were fears that WMDs were being transported secretly around Iraq in large tractor-trailer trucks. Several months before the war, a secret Defense Intelligence Agency mission in Iraq reported that large trailers captured by Kurdish troops did not, in fact, contain WMDs. However, when Secretary of State Colin Powell testified in front of the United Nations Security Council several months later, he stated that the United States had proof that biological weapons were being produced and transported in these trailers. Later, he would take back this statement. But, by then, the war had already begun.

The Beginning

As the clock ticked down, the gears of war continued to turn. On March 17, 2003, President Bush announced to Saddam Hussein that he had only forty-eight hours to leave Iraq with his family and allow the United States to help set a democratic election for a new ruler. If he did not leave, the United States would attack. American CIA teams had entered into Iraq months before, providing important intelligence for the ground troops who would follow. US General Tommy Franks was in charge of 248,000 soldiers from the United States, 45,000 British soldiers, 2,000 Australian soldiers, and 194 Polish soldiers. Approximately 70,000 Kurdish fighters, known as the peshmerga, also aided these forces.[8]

Transported to Kuwait, these troops awaited their orders. But Saddam Hussein did not leave, and the United States military received information that he and his family were staying in a village to the south of Baghdad. The coalition of the willing came up with a rapid plan to target Saddam Hussein, his sons Uday and Qusay, and approximately fifty other important Iraqi officials.

At 5:43 a.m. on March 20, 2003, without gaining approval from the UN Security Council first, the United States began the 2003 US-led invasion of Iraq, or what was to become known as Operation Iraqi Freedom.

5

OPERATION IRAQI FREEDOM

"I SENT AMERICAN TROOPS TO IRAQ TO MAKE ITS PEOPLE FREE, NOT TO MAKE THEM AMERICAN. IRAQIS WILL WRITE THEIR OWN HISTORY AND FIND THEIR OWN WAY."

—Former President George W. Bush[1]

As ground troops made their way from Kuwait into Iraq, coalition forces began airstrikes over Dora Farms on the outskirts of Baghdad. This is where the United States believed that Saddam Hussein was staying with his two sons in an underground bunker. Two fighter jets dropped four large bombs on a building there. At the same time, ships began to fire missiles. President Bush had hoped to end the war with this one attack. However, Saddam Hussein was not staying at Dora Farms.

In fact, he had not visited that location in many years. He had already begun to flee west across Iraq, but the United States and their allies did not know this. In this first attack in the invasion of Iraq, one Iraqi civilian was killed and fourteen others were wounded. For a while after the attack, the United States believed that Hussein had been killed. Then he appeared on Iraqi television to give a speech to the people of Iraq.

Airstrikes hit other targets in Baghdad and elsewhere in Iraq, too. Explosions could be heard everywhere. They called this "shock and awe," meaning that the coalition forces wanted to show Saddam Hussein and the people of Iraq the strength of their militaries and shock Hussein into giving up quickly. They hoped that by attacking a limited amount of targets—mostly top-ranking Iraqi officials—they would decrease civilian deaths and end the war quickly. However, not everything went according to plan.

Unforeseen Problems

Many Iraqi troops did not resist the coalition forces entering Iraq from Kuwait in the south. However, a special military group that remained loyal to Hussein, called Fedayeen Saddam, continued to fight against American and coalition forces. US forces had planned to head straight into central Iraq and Baghdad. But Fedayeen Saddam fighters hid in cities that coalition forces passed through and began surprise attacks. These surprise attacks are also known as guerilla-style attacks, where people hid in buildings and surprised the troops that passed by. This delayed many American troops from arriving in Baghdad for several weeks. Instead, they spent time fighting the Fedayeen in cities that they had expected to go through quickly.

There was also another problem for US forces: Turkey, the country to the north of Iraq, would not allow the US Army to pass through its territory. This meant that US forces would not be able to enter into Iraq from the north to join the fighting. However, US troops did end up parachuting into Turkey after all and met up with the Kurdish peshmerga forces to the north of Iraq in the beginning of April.

Iraqi Cities Fall

On April 4, US troops arrived in Baghdad and began to fight against the Republican Guard that was defending the capital city. They took control of the airport in Baghdad the same day. In less than a week, the Iraqi forces that had guarded the city collapsed. On April 9, US forces took control of Baghdad. On April 10, US forces captured another big city, Kirkuk, with the help of the peshmerga. On April 11, the large city of Mosul was captured. Saddam Hussein's hometown, Tikrit, fell on April 13. Soon, coalition forces controlled nearly all of Iraq, although smaller battles continued to occur.

When Baghdad fell, US forces helped a group of Iraqis to tear down a large statue of Saddam

Hussein in the center of the city. Journalists who watched took photos and videos, which would later become famous. Many Americans thought that the destruction of the statue showed that the Iraqis were glad the US military had come to Iraq. They didn't know that American soldiers first had the idea of tearing down the statue. While some Iraqis were glad that Saddam Hussein was gone, many were also afraid of what would come next. After the US military entered Baghdad, the city became chaotic. People snuck into governmental buildings and Hussein's palaces and stole anything they could find. A wave of crime swept over the city. There was mass panic.

History would prove that President Bush, who was making a speech on the aircraft carrier USS Abraham Lincoln, *was premature in his claims that it was "Mission Accomplished" in Iraq.*

Mission Accomplished

On May 1, President Bush flew out to an aircraft carrier off the coast of San Diego. The crew on this aircraft carrier had just returned from combat. In a televised speech, President Bush announced that major combat had ended in Iraq. A large banner that read "Mission Accomplished" hung behind him. It seemed as if the United States had won the war in just six weeks. Some people thought that the war was over, and that the people of Iraq and American soldiers would be safe. But many people thought that it was too soon to think that things would return to normal. They warned that more guerilla-style attacks could occur. They also warned that Saddam Hussein, who had gone into hiding, was not yet found. Until he was captured, many Iraqis still considered him their president.

The critics of President Bush's declaration would later be proved right. This early part of the American invasion would be the least violent part of the war. After President Bush's speech, fighting would intensify. In fact, most civilian and military deaths occurred after this early stage in the war. One hundred and fifty coalition soldiers had been killed by May 1, 2003. By November 2004, that number had increased to one thousand deaths.[2]

Hussein Is Found

Saddam Hussein remained in hiding for many months. He remained the top target for the US military. Many people claimed that they saw him throughout Iraq during the months after the American invasion, but he was never captured. In July, several months after the fall of Baghdad, US forces killed Saddam's two sons. Then, in December 2013, the US military got information

This photo allegedly shows Saddam Hussein following his capture.

that Hussein was hiding in a house in a village near his hometown of Tikrit. Six hundred soldiers were sent to ad-Dawr. They looked everywhere near a house where they believed Hussein was hiding. After several hours of searching, they nearly gave up. Then, finally, they found a small structure that covered a hole in the ground. Saddam Hussein was hiding inside. He came out with his hands up. "I am Saddam Hussein, the president of Iraq, and I am willing to negotiate," he said as he was taken away.[3]

By this point, the three-week war had turned into intense guerilla fighting. The United States struggled to help organize a new Iraqi government without Saddam Hussein and his party. This was more challenging than they had thought it would be. Many Iraqis grew angry that the American troops continued to stay in their country. Some of them joined the Fedayeen and other military groups. These groups fought together against coalition troops. The coalition called these groups "insurgents," which means that they were fighting against the democratic government that coalition forces were trying so hard to build.

The CPA and de-Baathification

When coalition forces had taken control of Baghdad, they set up the Coalition Provisional Authority (CPA). The CPA took control of the governing of Iraq until the Iraqi people could elect their own government. They set up the Green

Zone in central Baghdad, which was protected by concrete walls, barbed wire, and armed forces. This is also where American troops were housed. From the Green Zone, the CPA began issuing new laws. They encouraged foreign companies to invest in Iraq. They also hired American companies to rebuild Iraq's infrastructure. But the CPA's most controversial policy was called de-Baathification, which went into effect on May 16, 2003.

The Baath party had dominated the Iraqi government for nearly thirty-five years. Under Hussein's rule, if an Iraqi wanted to work for the state, he or she had to be a member of the Baath Party. Anyone who resisted becoming a member of this ruling party would be seen as suspicious. Some people who refused to join the Party were imprisoned, tortured, or killed. The CPA wanted to get rid of anyone in Iraq's government who could remain loyal to Saddam Hussein and his Baath Party. To do this, they began a policy of de-Baathification. Under the first part of this policy, any Iraqi who worked for the state and who had been a member of the Baath party was fired. They would no longer be allowed to work in any government job in Iraq. Very quickly, thousands of state employees found themselves with no job, no income, and little hope for the future. Between 50,000 and 100,000 doctors, civil servants, and teachers lost their jobs.[4]

The second stage of de-Baathification completely dissolved the Iraqi military.

Approximately 500,000 men who had fought for Saddam Hussein lost their jobs and their salaries.[5] These men were later tempted, using weapons they still owned from the dissolved Iraqi military, to fight against American troops.

Michael Aflaq was the secretary general of the Baath party.

One of the main problems with de-Baathification was that it disenfranchised large groups of previously powerful Sunnis. Saddam Hussein and most Baath party members were Sunni Muslims. Under Hussein's rule, there were some tensions between Sunni and Shia Muslims. This was because, while Hussein as a Sunni led the country, most Iraqis are Shia. In fact, Sunnis only make up about 35 percent of the population of Iraq, while Shia make up 65 percent.[6] Saddam Hussein was afraid that the Shia population would rise up against him. During his rule, he removed the Shia from prominent positions and brutally crushed any Shia uprisings, killing many of his own citizens. These tensions flared up again during the de-Baathification

Muqtada al-Sadr is the leader of the radical Mahdi Army.

process. Because many Sunnis and Baathists were not allowed to stay in public and government positions, they grew angry and resentful. The CPA focused on giving the long- repressed Shia and Kurdish populations more representation in government. This, too, made many Sunnis feel like they would have no active role in the new government.

The Insurgency Begins

With no job and no money, many former Baath party members and Sunni radicals began to join the insurgency. Members of Hussein's military who were banned from joining the new military also joined these insurgent groups. The insurgents promised these men a good salary and food and housing for their families. It was very tempting for them to fight against the Americans.

These insurgent groups and militias targeted American soldiers and Iraqis who fought for the coalition government. Much of this fighting took place in the Sunni Triangle of Iraq, an area to the northwest of Baghdad where a large Sunni population lived in several large cities. The insurgency used guerilla fighting, ambushes, suicide bombings, and planted mortars and improvised explosive devices (IEDs). They hid IEDs near roads where coalition forces would drive, and set these devices off at a distance with their cell phones. Many American and coalition soldiers were killed in this way.

Sunnis and Shia

In the spring of 2004, fighting increased not only between Sunni militias and coalition forces, but also between radical Shia groups and the coalition. Although the Shia population held more power in the Iraqi government than when Hussein was in power, some Shias did not want American forces to stay in Iraq. These radicals believed that American forces were occupying their country, and that western influence was evil. Soon, a Shia cleric named Muqtada al-Sadr created a militia called the Mahdi Army. The Mahdi Army was made up mostly of young, religious students who lived and studied in a poor section of Baghdad called Sadr

The Abu Ghraib prison was the site of human rights violations by the US military against prisoners there.

city. At first, al-Sadr led this group of men to critique American involvement in Iraq without violence. However, in April 2004, the American military closed al-Sadr's newspaper and arrested one of his top aids. Al-Sadr delivered a fiery sermon to his students, and the Mahdi Army was created.

Throughout the spring of 2004, Mahdi militiamen fought against US forces and the US-trained Iraqi army. Intense fighting began as the militia took over important Shia cities in the south of Iraq. A brief truce began in June, but it did not last long. Fighting continued throughout the summer.

Also in 2004, attacks against Shias began to increase. This led to an increase in tension not only between Iraqis and Americans, but between different religious groups in Iraq as well. In May 2004, on a Shia holy day called Ashura, bombs were set off at important shrines in Baghdad and Karbala. Karbala is an important religious site for Shia Muslims. That day, 180 worshipping Shia were killed in the bombings.[7] The United States stated that the attacks were by an Al Qaeda group in Iraq, led by a man named Abu Musab al-Zarqawi. But many Shia Muslims blamed the United States. They said that the United States had invaded their country and had promised to protect them, but wasn't keeping their promises.

Abu Ghraib

More criticism was directed at the American government in April 2004. This was when photos of prisoners being tortured and abused in Abu Ghraib came to light. Abu Ghraib is a prison that was used by Saddam Hussein during his presidency. He kept many people there who spoke out, or who were accused of speaking out, against his government. Many Iraqi prisoners were tortured and killed. After the US invasion, the American military took over the prison complex. Thousands of prisoners who fought against coalition forces were kept there.

But some journalists and human rights organizations spoke of human rights abuses at

Abu Ghraib. They said that Iraqi prisoners were protesting how they were being treated. These prisoners said that they were held without receiving fair trials and were abused. Prisoners described being tortured with heat and electricity, not being allowed to wear clothes, and not being allowed to sleep. Some Iraqis in Abu Ghraib even went missing.

Then photos were published showing the torture of these Iraqi prisoners. These photos were widely published. The US military dishonorably discharged the men and women in the photos shown abusing Iraqi prisoners and, later, put them on trial. Two of the soldiers were sentenced to multiple years in prison. But critics of US policy

Prime Minister Iyad Allawi speaks to Iraqi troops during a camp visit in Fallujah in November 2004.

towards Iraqi prisoners said that it wasn't the fault of just these individual soldiers. They said that it was part of a larger problem. They accused the American government of knowing about the use of torture, and even encouraging it. This caused more anger against American troops amongst Iraqis and led to increased violence.

The Interim Government

Soon after the Abu Ghraib scandal shook American military power in Iraq, the coalition handed over power to an interim Iraqi government. The prime minister of this interim government was a man named Iyad Allawi. Coalition forces hoped that the interim government would govern until the Iraqi people could democratically elect a new government. They set elections for January 30, 2005.

The First Battle of Fallujah

But the insurgency in Iraq did not get better during this time. In fact, it got worse, especially in one city in Iraq: Fallujah. Fallujah is a city with a large Sunni population in Iraq's Sunni Triangle. Many supporters of Saddam Hussein and the Baath Party lived there. Even from the beginning of the war, many Iraqis in Fallujah protested against the American invasion. In the early part of the war, residents marched in protest of the US invasion. American soldiers fired on the crowd, killing a number of civilians. This began a series of attacks on coalition forces in and around Fallujah.

Then, in March 2004, four military contractors were ambushed and killed in Fallujah. The US military continued airstrikes on the city and struggled to regain control. They wanted to capture the men responsible for killing these Americans and to chase the insurgents out of the city. This was called the First Battle of Fallujah, and it would last less than a month. While the US military won this battle, they lost the war of public opinion. Many Iraqi civilians were killed during the First Battle of Fallujah. Government reports have estimated that about six hundred Iraqi civilians, two hundred insurgents, and twenty-seven American soldiers were killed. Some witnesses claim to have seen American soldiers firing on ambulances carrying civilians. The US military claimed that insurgents were hiding in these ambulances, while many Iraqis claimed that the US military specifically targeted civilians. Many Iraqis—and many Americans, too—felt that the war had gone too far.

Then, in November 2004, the interim Iraqi government along with US and British forces began what would be known as "Operation Phantom Fury." They wanted to force out insurgency groups that still held power in Fallujah. After the first battle in April, insurgents had gradually taken over the city once again. This new battle became known as the Second Battle of Fallujah. Once again, Fallujah fell to ruin in the deadliest fighting of the war. These battles marked a turning point in the Iraq War: For the first time, the Iraqi government and coalition forces fought against insurgents rather than against Baathist supporters and Hussein loyalists. The US military's enemies in Iraq were shifting, which signaled that the war was far from over.

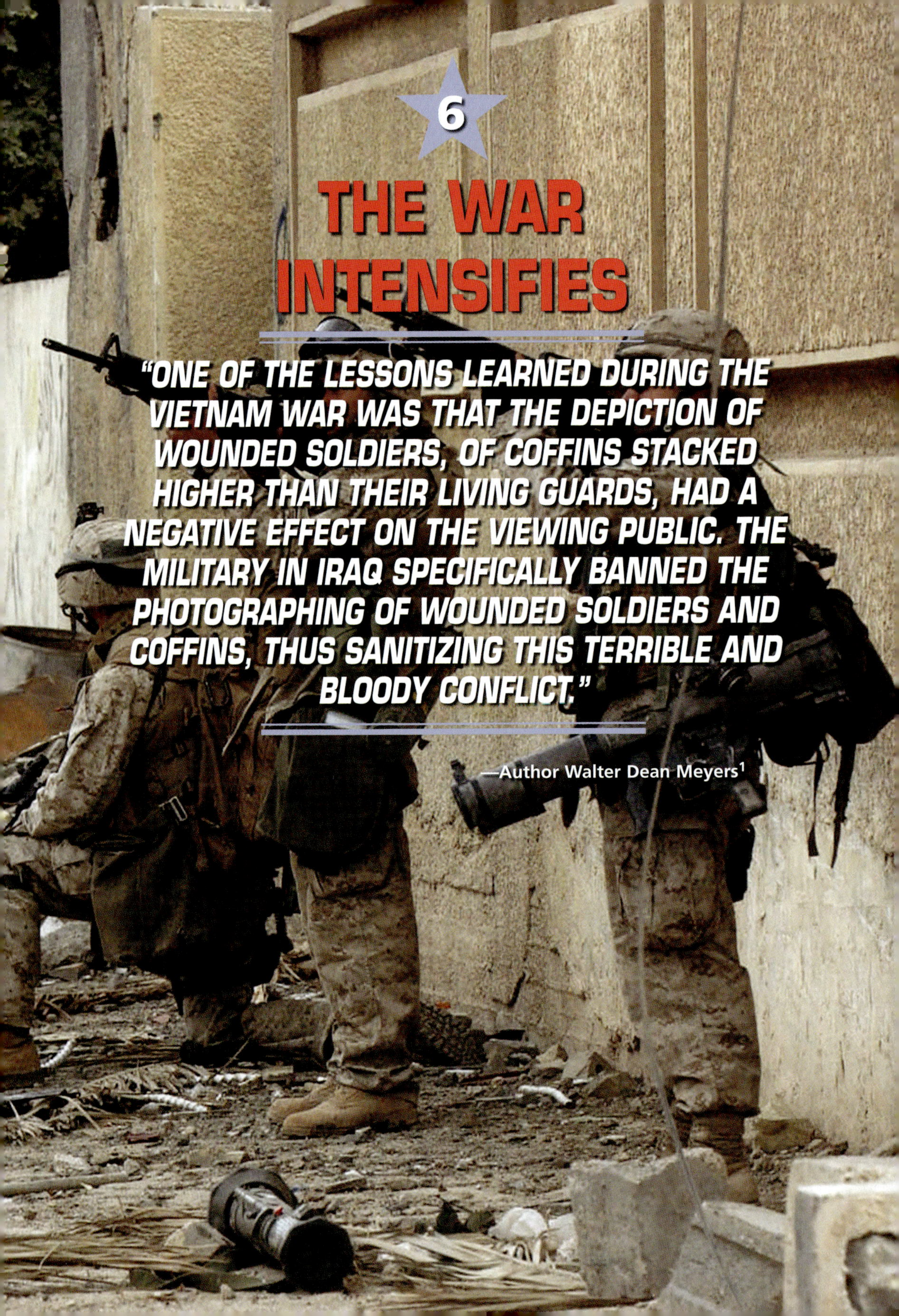

6

THE WAR INTENSIFIES

"ONE OF THE LESSONS LEARNED DURING THE VIETNAM WAR WAS THAT THE DEPICTION OF WOUNDED SOLDIERS, OF COFFINS STACKED HIGHER THAN THEIR LIVING GUARDS, HAD A NEGATIVE EFFECT ON THE VIEWING PUBLIC. THE MILITARY IN IRAQ SPECIFICALLY BANNED THE PHOTOGRAPHING OF WOUNDED SOLDIERS AND COFFINS, THUS SANITIZING THIS TERRIBLE AND BLOODY CONFLICT."

—Author Walter Dean Meyers[1]

The Second Battle of Fallujah began on November 7, 2004. This battle would become the bloodiest that American troops had seen since the Vietnam War thirty years earlier. US forces had cleared the large city of people who were loyal to the Baath Party during the First Battle of Fallujah. But now the city had fallen to insurgents. These insurgents did not want to restore Saddam Hussein to power. Rather, they were just trying to destabilize the Iraqi regime.

On November 7, 2004, four marine and two army battalions joined together to finally get rid of the insurgents in Fallujah. Over fifteen thousand soldiers joined with Iraqi security forces.[2] They entered the city from the west and south with the help of air strikes against insurgent positions. Within twenty-four hours, they had secured Fallujah hospital and all major bridges leading into and out of the city. The initial plan had worked: to create a diversion while more marines entered Fallujah from the north. US forces waited while air strikes continued before beginning the ground assault.

During the night of November 8, the ground assault began. The marine and army battalions began to push into Fallujah from their positions at the northern edge of the city. They were met with IEDs, rocket-propelled grenades, and gunfire. Their enemies were so close that it was hard to tell if someone walking nearby was trying to help them or kill them. One of the most difficult areas to clear was an area called the Jolan district. Many insurgents were active in this area. Insurgents hid in homes and on top of buildings; their attacks often took US and Iraqi forces by surprise.

Greg Nichols, a marine who took part in the fighting, described it this way: "[W]e were on vehicles. But, you know . . . the guys that are on the ground . . . are doing the house-to-house fighting . . . The only way that you can actually engage and take territory is to put boots . . . in that house, in that room, in that window. I mean, it was just really very close, very violent, very intense."[3]

Insurgents had known that coalition forces would be attacking Fallujah. They booby-trapped buildings and planted bombs in cars. They also dug tunnels and barriers to help hide themselves. They built a large number of IEDs that they hid throughout the city. All of this made the fighting more intense and violent than any previous battle in the war.

The most intense fighting occurred around the Jolan district. Approaching this district, 19 marines were killed and 245 were injured.[4] Following heavy and close fighting, US forces cleared this area. After this, the worst fighting was over. US forces continued to fight isolated groups of insurgents, but they had taken over most areas of the city. By the end of December, the battle was won. Once again, US forces had cleared Fallujah of insurgents.

The Second Battle of Fallujah claimed 119 American, British, and Iraqi lives, and left 613 soldiers injured. Although there are no official statistics, experts believe that between 1,500 and 2,000 insurgents were killed. The Red Cross has stated that 800 civilians were killed during the fighting as well.[5]

Human Rights Abuses

Later on, troubling accounts came out about the fighting in Fallujah. In particular, some journalists stated that the devastation of the war was not being accurately portrayed, especially in regard to the large amount of civilian deaths. In 2004, American journalist Rahul Mahajan stated that many of the Iraqi civilians who were killed were women and children. These reports were often reported in Arab media networks such as Al-Jazeera and were not broadcast by major American networks.

Noam Chomsky, a well-known media critic, also criticized major media networks for not covering human rights abuses in Iraq. American forces were accused of deliberately killing civilians and of using the chemical agent white phosphorous against insurgents. The United States has maintained that it never used white phosphorous, a chemical weapon that burns anything it touches, even though various international media outlets, including the BBC, have aired reports with eye-witness testimony from both Iraqi civilians and American military forces that the chemical weapon had been used.

The Beginning of the Civil Conflict

The Second Battle of Fallujah also proved to be a turning point in the war for another reason. Between 2006 and 2007, fighting between different religious groups within Iraq would increase. Some experts have called this period a civil war, although many prefer to call it a civil conflict instead. The American military called this period "the surge," because they needed to send many more troops into Iraq to deal with the increased violence.

After this battle, the city of Fallujah was almost entirely destroyed. Many buildings were blown up and coalition bulldozers ripped up roads as they entered into the city. Over the next couple of years, Iraqi and coalition forces rebuilt the city. Civilians returned slowly to their houses, although many of Fallujah's residents never returned to their destroyed city.

However, with increased violence breaking out in 2006, Fallujah was again a hotbed of violence. Most of the gains that had been achieved during the Second Battle of Fallujah were lost. The city once again fell into the hands of insurgents.

Parliamentary Elections

But there was some hope, too. The first democratic elections held in fifty years in Iraq were scheduled for January 30, 2005. Iraqi citizens would elect a new Iraqi parliament, whose major task would be to write a new constitution for the nation. Before the elections, there were many threats that voting stations would be bombed. But, in a show of bravery and strength, Iraqi citizens were not deterred. Despite the threats of violence from insurgency groups, many Iraqis voted for the first time in their lives. They proudly displayed the purple ink on their index fingers—a

An Iraqi woman casts her ballot, holding up her ink-stained finger, at the first election after Saddam Hussein's fall.

sign that they had voted that was used to prevent repeat voting—after emerging from the voting stations. This was one of the first steps in a long process to return power to the Iraqis so they could begin governing themselves again.

The International Mission for Iraqi Elections, an international group made up of nine different nations, monitored the elections. They made sure the election results were accurate and that no one had tampered with the votes. Coalition forces and Iraqi security forces guarded voting stations to prevent terrorist attacks and to allow citizens to safely reach the polling stations to cast their votes. Terrorist groups such as Al Qaeda threatened to prevent elections by suicide bombings and other attacks against voters. However, security forces managed to prevent many attacks on voting stations. Even so, there were more than one hundred attacks on election day that killed forty-four people.[6] The people who were killed had known about the threat of violence and had decided to vote anyway. This was how important voting, and taking back control of their government, was to the people of Iraq.

Aside from the threat of violence, there was another problem that occurred during these elections. Sunni Muslims are a minority population in Iraq, although they had been in power for many years under Saddam Hussein. The Shias, however, are the religious majority. Many Sunnis were worried that they would lose power in government during elections because they did not represent the largest religious group in the country. Sunni leaders called on their fellow Sunnis to boycott the elections. This means that they would intentionally not vote in order to protest what they viewed as their exclusion from the new government. Some Sunnis also chose to boycott due to the threat of violence. However, this made the situation for Sunnis worse. Although Sunnis make up approximately 30 percent of the population in Iraq, the largest Sunni political party only received less than 2 percent of the vote.[7] By choosing not to vote, they had made their worst fears come to pass. Shia and Kurdish parties earned the majority of the votes, because they actually came out and voted. Many people said that the vote was unfair because of the Sunni boycott and the results were not representative of the Iraqi population. This would reoccur in later elections and would be a continuing source of problems for the new government of Iraq.

Following the election in January 2005, a new constitution was drawn up. In December 2005, new parliamentary elections were held. Compared to the elections held less than a year before, there were fewer threats of violence. More Sunnis were represented in this vote as well, which was a promising sign. After the elections, a coalition government was built around the newly elected prime minister, a Shia named Nouri al-Maliki. The goal of this new government was to stabilize Iraq and prevent the country from descending into civil war. However, Iraq's movement toward civil conflict had already begun and would not be easily stopped. People had been repressed and brutalized for so long, it was hard to work with other opposing groups in the nation to create a functioning government that worked for everyone and let go of political and religious tensions enough to establish a lasting peace.

7

THE CIVIL CONFLICT AND THE SURGE

"I REPEAT MY DEMAND THAT THE OCCUPIER LEAVE THE LAND OF OUR BELOVED IRAQ UNCONDITIONALLY, WITHOUT RETAINING BASES OR SIGNING AGREEMENTS."

—Shia Cleric Moqtada al-Sadr[1]

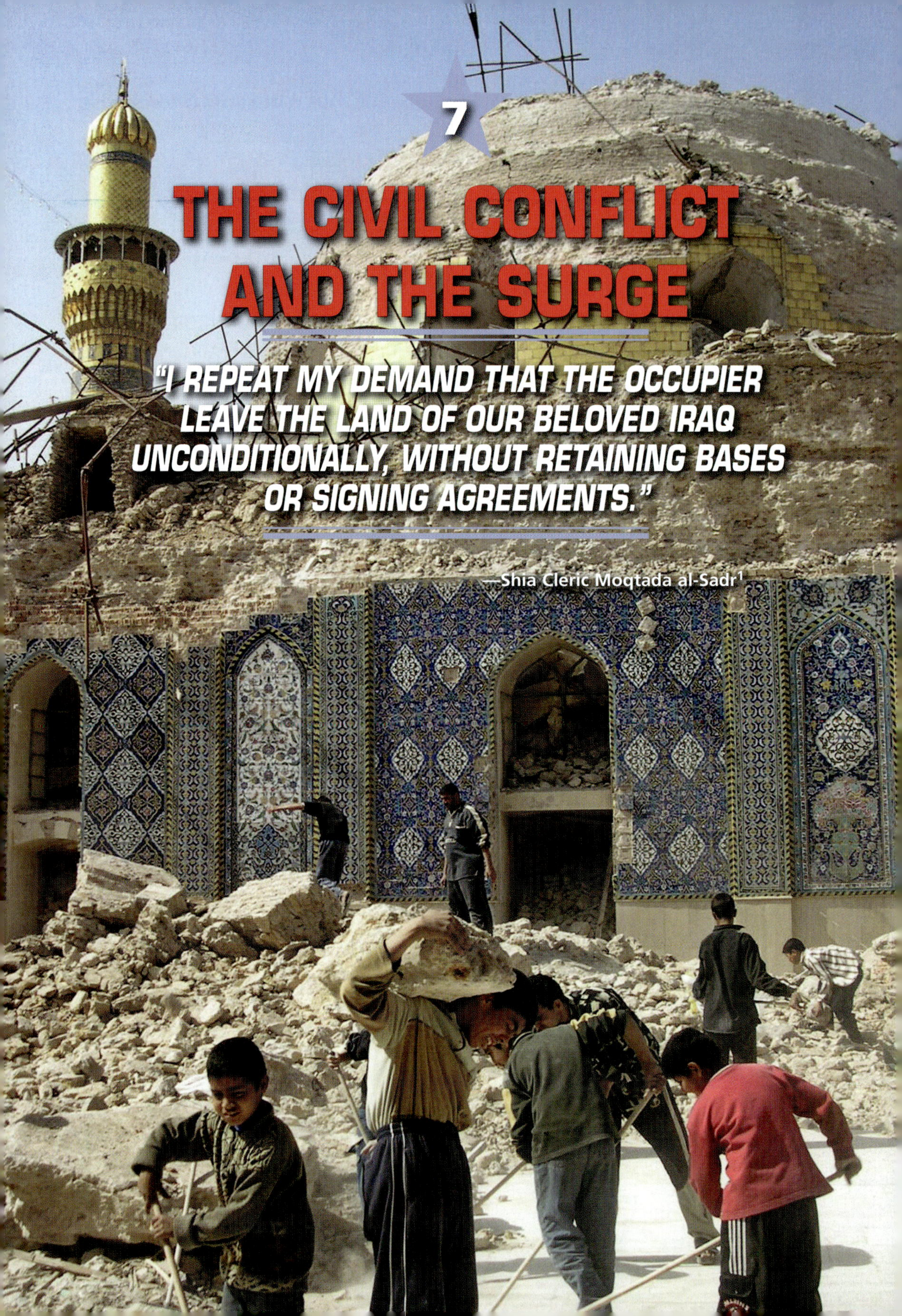

As Iraq descended into increased violence toward the end of 2005, a horrible attack occurred in a city named Haditha. On November 19, 2005, American forces killed twenty-four unarmed Iraqi civilians. Earlier that day, an IED exploded and killed Lance Corporal Miguel Terazzas. Initially, US forces stated that fifteen Iraqis had been killed with Terazzas by the IED that day. Later, journalists discovered evidence that this was not true. They found that, after Terazzas's death, a group of marines went on a rampage in Haditha.

They entered into families' homes and deliberately killed men, women, and children. For many involved in the Iraq War, this was a sign of the terrible turn the war was taking. Iraqi civilians were being killed in retaliation for American deaths inflicted by insurgents. It also showed the psychological trauma the war had caused for the marines who went on this rampage. According to journalist Tim McGirk, "What happened in Haditha is a reminder of the horrors faced by civilians caught in the middle of war—and what war can do to the people who fight it."[2]

After a six-year investigation, charges against the seven marines involved in the massacre were largely dropped. None of those responsible for the massacre were sentenced to jail time. For many Iraqis, this was devastating. To them, it showed that American forces could act with impunity against innocent Iraqi civilians. Conditions were deteriorating in Iraq, especially among different religious groups and American forces. According to a *Time* magazine poll, 85 percent of Sunnis were against coalition forces in Iraq, while 65 percent of Iraqis overall agreed that coalition forces should leave their country.[3]

Rise in Sectarianism

Then, another devastating attack occurred. On February 22, 2006, a bomb went off in an important Shia shrine in Samarra, a holy city north of Baghdad. The Askariyya shrine is a holy site for

Shias and one of the most important Shia sites in the world. It was built in 944 CE and houses the remains of two imams, or important Shia spiritual leaders. The bomb destroyed the shrine's golden dome. Although no injuries were reported after the bombing, this was a devastating blow to the Shia community in Iraq. They felt that their religion and way of life was under attack. No group claimed responsibility for the attack, although many believed that the Sunni group Al Qaeda was responsible.

The Askariyya bombing set off a new wave of violence in Iraq. In fact, many would later state that this was an important moment that would set off increasing sectarianism. In the days following the bombing, 168 mosques were attacked.[4] Ten imams were murdered and fifteen were kidnapped. Some Shias sought revenge by attacking Sunnis, while Sunnis fought back against the Shias. The prime minister called for several days of national mourning. He called out for Iraqis to remain united, despite religious differences. But this would not occur. Sunni groups like Al Qaeda in Iraq continued bombings and suicide attacks against both American and Shia targets. The Mahdi Army renewed attacks against Sunnis, as well, primarily through death squads that kidnapped, tortured, and killed targets.

During this time, many Iraqi civilians who had lived through the early stages of the war were displaced. The United Nations has calculated that, during this period of time, two million Iraqis were forced to leave their homes in Iraq and move elsewhere within the country. There were also 2.7 million Iraqis who were forced to leave Iraq and move to other countries as political refugees.[5] Many of these refugees were civilians who were targeted because of their religious affiliation and many of them were religious minorities such as Christians.

It seemed as if the country had broken apart. Iraqis with different religious backgrounds who had lived together in relative peace for many years now feared for their lives. Experts stated that this was due to the destabilization of Iraq following the American invasion, as well as coalition policies like de-Baathification. Whatever it was, Iraq was worse off now than it had been during the beginning of the war in 2003. The Iraqi government, with the aid of coalition forces, desperately sought a way to end the violence.

Saddam Hussein's Execution

At the end of 2006, Saddam Hussein was hanged for crimes against humanity after being found guilty by an Iraqi court. He was convicted of killing 148 men and boys in the Shia city of Dujail in 1982, following a failed assassination attempt on him. The sentence was carried out on an American military base north of Baghdad and was recorded secretly on a cell phone. The disturbing images of his execution were broadcast around the world.

Following his death, President Bush gave a speech. He stated, "Saddam Hussein's execution comes at the end of a difficult year for the Iraqi people and for our troops. Bringing Saddam Hussein to justice will not end the violence in Iraq, but it is an important milestone on Iraq's course to becoming a democracy that can govern, sustain and defend itself, and be an ally in the war on terror."[6]

The Surge

Iraq's descent into civil conflict and sectarianism continued. The day after Saddam Hussein's execution, on December 31, 2006, American military deaths reached three thousand. This was a somber reminder of the price coalition forces were paying by remaining in Iraq.

In January 2007, President Bush announced a new plan. Additional American troops would be sent to Iraq. This was called "the surge," or, officially, "The New Way Forward." Twenty thousand soldiers were deployed and sent into Iraq, mostly to Baghdad and some to Sunni-populated areas in the northwest of Iraq. President Bush stated that he hoped that American soldiers would help suppress the sectarianism that had grown in Iraq. He wanted American soldiers to work with the Iraqi military to protect Iraqi citizens, while letting Iraqis lead their own country. While the surge had many supporters, many politicians disagreed with putting more American lives in danger. They called

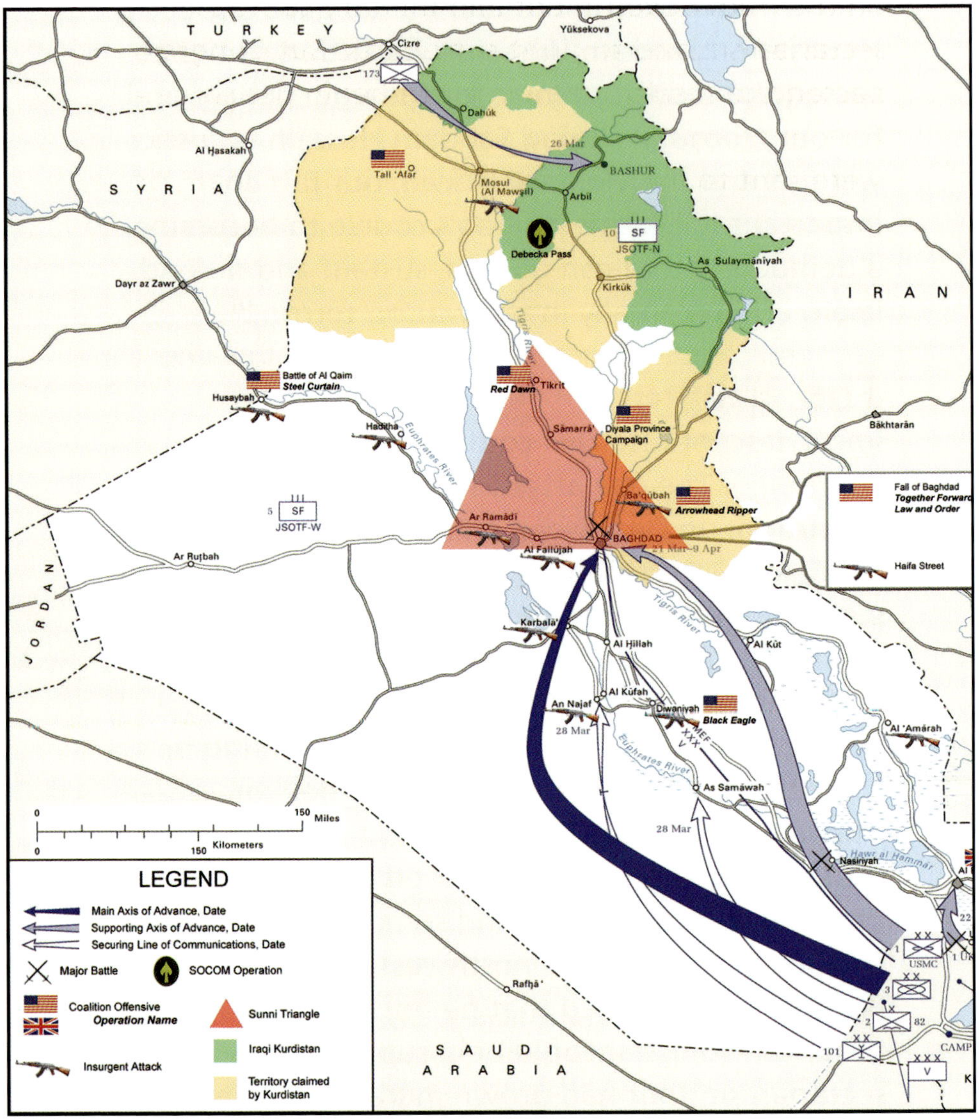

This map shows the location of Iraqi and US forces in Iraq in 2007. The Sunni triangle is in red.

on the Iraqi government and military to stop sectarianism and to fight extremists. But Congress passed the resolution needed to begin the surge. Between January and May, thousands of soldiers were sent to Iraq. Despite the increase in coalition troops in and near Baghdad, security decreased and deaths increased. During this period of time, nearly two thousand Iraqi civilians were killed each month on average.[7] The year 2007 became the deadliest year for American soldiers in Iraq since 2004.

The Sunni Awakening

Soon, American military commanders had a new plan. They had been previously working with some Shia military groups to fight against Sunni insurgents. But, with the increase in conflict between Shias and Sunnis, they didn't want to contribute to growing sectarianism. Instead, the American military began to arm moderate Sunni military groups against radical Sunni organizations like Al Qaeda. This was a very controversial plan. Many critics of the plan stated that large numbers of the Sunni military groups that the American military wanted to arm had previously attacked and killed coalition troops. They said that there was no guarantee that, once armed, they would fight against the extremists. Instead, they could use American weapons against American troops. Even more worrisome, some of the groups that the American military

Sunni leaders meet with the Iraqi government here to discuss rebuilding areas that were damaged during fighting between insurgents and US soldiers.

wanted to arm against Al Qaeda had previous ties with the Islamist group. It was hard to tell whose side each group was on. And it was a big risk to arm these groups without knowing if they would follow through with the plan.

In addition to this, it wasn't easy for American troops to convince some Sunni tribal groups to fight against other Sunnis. American troops met with Sunni sheikhs in small groups. They needed to offer something in return for their support. But, with negotiation, a deal was reached with many tribes. Sunni sheikhs would lead their tribal militias against Al Qaeda in exchange for weapons, cash, and political influence in the new government. According to a 2011 report, the American military spent three hundred million dollars for Sunni support.[8] But this would prove to be a successful military strategy. This was called the Sunni Awakening, and it would change the course of the Iraq War.

Sunni sheikhs formed alliances with one another with the help of coalition forces and the Iraqi military. They became known as the Sons of Iraq. In addition to fighting against Al Qaeda, they promised to no longer fight against coalition forces and Iraqi security. They also promised to patrol their neighborhoods to increase security around Iraq. The Sunni Awakening was largely successful and Al Qaeda was pushed out of its previous stronghold in Iraq.

In September 2008, American forces formally returned security responsibility to the Iraqi military. This was definitive proof of the success of the Sunni Awakening in just over one year. Soon, this success also led to plans to withdraw large numbers of American troops from Iraq by 2009, with full withdrawal set for 2011. Once again, Americans and Iraqis called for an end to the war. This time, it seemed like these calls would be answered.

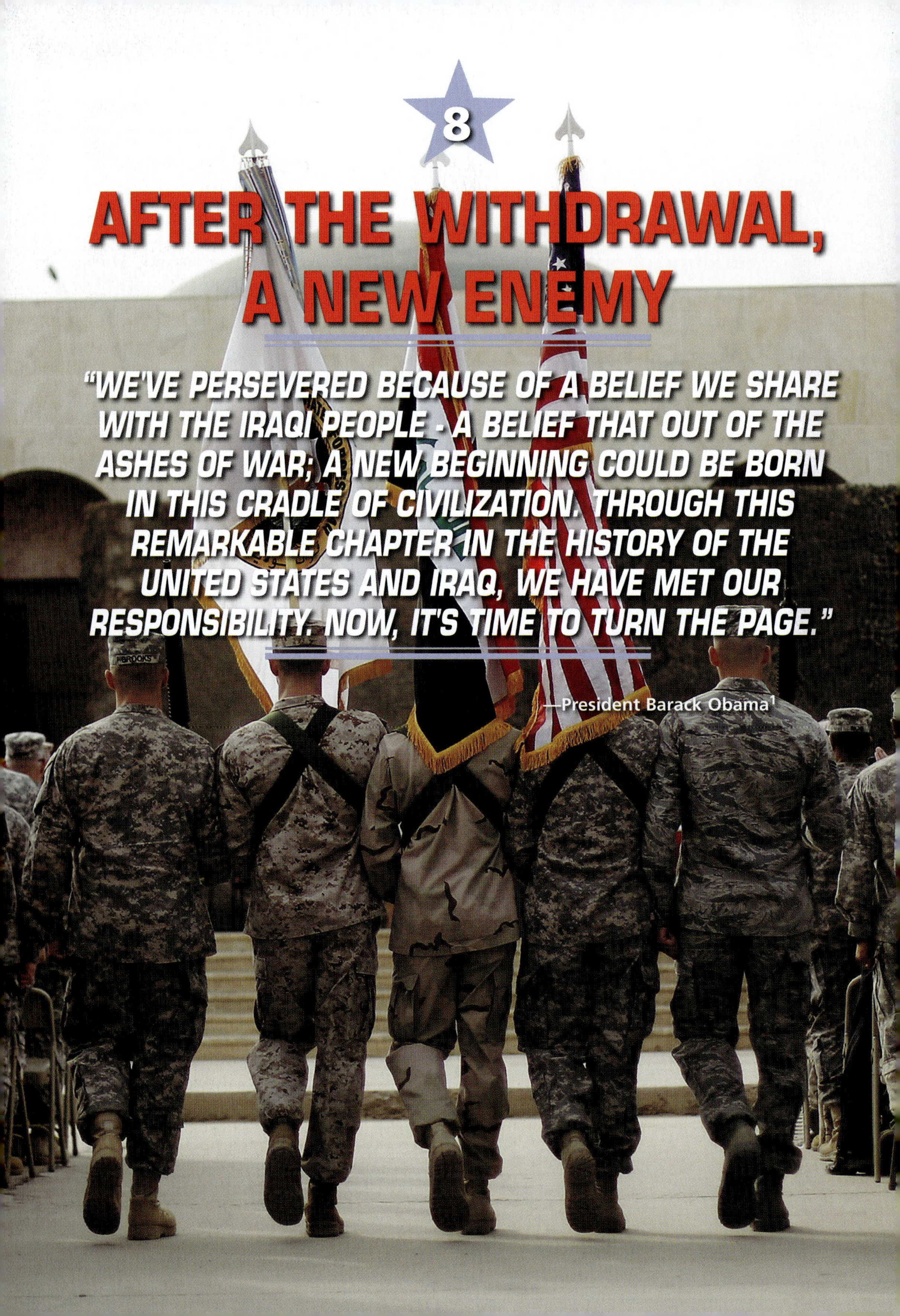

8

AFTER THE WITHDRAWAL, A NEW ENEMY

"WE'VE PERSEVERED BECAUSE OF A BELIEF WE SHARE WITH THE IRAQI PEOPLE - A BELIEF THAT OUT OF THE ASHES OF WAR; A NEW BEGINNING COULD BE BORN IN THIS CRADLE OF CIVILIZATION. THROUGH THIS REMARKABLE CHAPTER IN THE HISTORY OF THE UNITED STATES AND IRAQ, WE HAVE MET OUR RESPONSIBILITY. NOW, IT'S TIME TO TURN THE PAGE."

—President Barack Obama[1]

After announcements that American troops would withdraw, there were celebrations in the streets of Iraq. Americans celebrated at home, too. By 2008, American casualties had reached four thousand in the Iraq War.[2] Americans were tired of losing people as the war dragged on. It seemed like both sides were willing and ready to end the war.

While bombings still killed Iraqi civilians throughout 2009, the country was generally stabilized. In January 2009, Iraqi civilian casualties were the lowest ever at 191.[3]

This was compared to more than two thousand deaths per month at the height of fighting in 2006. At the end of May, the last British troops left Iraq. By the end of the year, the lowest recorded number of American deaths in Iraq since the beginning of the war was recorded.

Prime Minister al-Maliki

In March 2010, a new parliamentary election led to the reelection of Nouri al-Maliki as prime minister of Iraq. Al-Maliki was known as a conservative Shia politician. Sunni Iraqis accused him of inflaming sectarian feelings in the Iraqi government. Some people stated that he did not care about continuing to support both Sunni and Shia Iraqi civilians. This would become problematic. As al-Maliki continued as the head of his government, he began to disband the Sons of Iraq. Some stated that it was because he did not want to continue to support Sunni tribes. Others accused al-Maliki more pointedly. They grew angry when he arrested a prominent Sunni tribal leader and sentenced him to death. To these critics of al-Maliki's government, the prime minister was pitting Shias against Sunnis. Whether or not this was the case, from 2010 through 2012 al-Maliki dissolved many of the Sunni Awakening groups.

End of Combat Missions

In August 2010, President Barack Obama declared an end to all combat missions in Iraq. In his speech from the Oval Office, broadcast around the United States, President Obama said that America would continue to help Iraq as the country established democracy and worked toward continued peace.

President Obama stated that it was time for the Iraqis to govern their own country without the help of the American military. It seemed as if the long, seven-year war had come to an end. Most Americans were very happy with this decision. Some Americans remained critical of President Obama's plan, however. They wanted to keep some American troops in Iraq for security purposes. These troops would guarantee that Iraq would not descend into violence again and lose all of the gains that had been made through the sacrifice of so many American soldiers. They warned that Iraq was perhaps not as stable as it appeared to be.

One year after his speech announcing the end of combat missions, President Obama announced that the last American soldiers would leave Iraq by the end of 2011. This would officially bring the war to a close. The Iraq War had lasted nearly nine years, and 4,493 American troops had lost their lives.[4] The United States had paid more than one trillion dollars to support it. On December 15, 2011, a formal ceremony was held in Baghdad as American troops left the country. All across Iraq, American military officers handed over the keys to former American military bases to Iraqi officials.

Prime Minister al-Maliki speaks at a press conference on the timing of American troop withdrawal.

Marginalized Sunnis

Rafi al-Essawi, the minister of finance of Iraq during this time, stated that Iraqis thought that the nation would come together after the Americans left. But this isn't what happened. Instead, relationships began to deteriorate between different religious groups and violence increased. According to al-Essawi and others, Prime Minister al-Maliki didn't fulfill his promise to making Iraq's government more inclusive. Instead, he seemed to start a campaign to take many prominent Sunnis out of powerful positions in the government and the military.

The sectarianism that al-Maliki publicly vowed to fight against started to grow in his administration. He got rid of many Sunni politicians who disagreed with him. Many Iraqis, especially Sunni Iraqis, wanted to keep the Sons of Iraq as a military force in the country. They stated that, although Al Qaeda had been forced out of the country, there was no guarantee they wouldn't return. Keeping the Sunni tribal militias would be a good guarantee against any Sunni extremist groups gaining power in the country.

The American government urged al-Maliki to continue paying the Sons of Iraq so they would be encouraged to keep fighting for their country. But al-Maliki soon put restrictions on recruitment and pay. Salaries decreased and many militia fighters felt that they weren't valued. Soon, many Sons of Iraq fighters had left the militia. To some Sunnis, it seemed as if al-Maliki was suspicious of them. He wanted to keep power in the hands of his own party and took it away from these militia groups.

Sunnis like Rafi al-Essawi also claimed that the al-Maliki administration discriminated against Sunnis. Al-Maliki stated that he did this for security reasons, but Sunnis felt that they were being unfairly punished. Every time there was an attack in Iraq, al-Essawi said, Sunnis were blamed. Government cars would arrive on the scene and arrest hundreds of Sunnis for no other reason than they had been present at the time of the attack. These people were held in prison for months or even years. They did not receive trials.

Tariq al-Hashemi, a Sunni Iraqi who served as vice president in al-Maliki's government, summed up how many Sunnis felt: "To be an Arab Sunni in Iraq, you're a terrorist. Simple as that."[5]

By late 2012, large numbers of Sunnis began to protest across Iraq. They wanted al-Maliki to resign. The Iraqi government sent forces into these protest areas and sometimes civilians were killed. This caused more animosity between religious groups in the country.

The Arab Spring

As protests spread across Iraq, protests developed across the larger Middle East as well. In December of 2010, Arab Spring protests began in Tunisia, following the death of Mohamed Bouazizi, who set himself on fire in protest of police harassment. Many young people across the Middle East were tired of the way they were being treated by their governments. They got out into the streets and demanded change. These protests spread quickly through North Africa and the Middle East, resulting in political unrest. Several Arab governments were overthrown, including the Tunisian, Egyptian, and Yemini presidents. Civil wars began in Libya and Syria. The situation got even worse in 2012 and 2013 during the Syrian civil war, when various paramilitary groups formed with the hopes of deposing the despotic President Bashar al-Assad.

This proved to be the perfect storm. Young Sunni men, feeling that they were discriminated against by al-Maliki's government, crossed over the northwestern border of Iraq into Syria. Islamist groups such as Al Qaeda radicalized these men. They gave them weapons, food, and money in exchange for their promise to fight against those loyal to al-Assad and anyone they claimed to be infidels.

Sectarian and Ethnic Violence

In 2013, Sunni militants involved in the Syrian civil war, hoping to utilize the sectarian conflict in Iraq to their advantage, intensified attacks against Iraq's Shia population. The civil war in Syria, combined with the destabilization of Iraq caused by the American invasion, caused some of the worst sectarian violence seen in years. For quite some time, Iraqis with different religious beliefs and traditions existed together peacefully. As Islamist groups grew more powerful, however, they threatened anyone who did not follow their radical religious beliefs.

Sunni militant groups also increased attacks against minority populations within Iraq, such as the Assyrians and Yazidis. Assyrians are the native people of Iraq who speak an ancient language called Aramaic. They are the third-largest ethnic group in Iraq, following the Arabs and the Kurds, and are predominantly Christian. The Yazidis are mostly Kurdish, which means that they do not consider themselves Arab. However, unlike the majority of Kurds, Yazidis are not Sunni Muslims. Instead, Yazidis follow their own ancient religion,

Yazdânism, which incorporates beliefs from Christianity, Judaism, and Islam.

Following the invasion, violence against Iraqi Assyrians and Christians increased, with many instances of abductions, tortures, and bombings reported. Clergymen, such as the Archbishop Paulos Faraj Rahho, the Archbishop of Mosul, were killed after abductions despite payments of ransoms. Many religious minority groups fled Iraq. More than half of all Assyrians, who had once numbered 6 percent of the population, left their country in fear of their lives.[6]

The Rise of the Islamic State

As Al Qaeda grew in Syria during the civil war, a new branch of the extremist group emerged. This group was even more violent than Al Qaeda. They called themselves the Islamic State of Iraq and Syria (ISIS), and their goal was to create their own government, a Sunni caliphate, in Syrian and Iraqi territory. Many experts blame al-Maliki's policies against Sunni Iraqis for the rise of ISIS. But ISIS grew powerful due to a "perfect storm" of events around the globe. The US-led invasion of Iraq and the CPA's policy of de-Baathification disenfranchised many Iraqis, particularly Sunni Muslims. Prime Minister al-Maliki's policies further angered Sunni Muslims. They felt that they had no voice in the new Iraqi government and that their demands would not be met. Most Iraqi Sunnis did not turn to violence to have their voices heard, but a

An ISIS fighter waves the ISIS flag from a captured military plane.

minority did. However, ISIS still would not have become so powerful without another important political event: the Arab Spring. After many years of fighting during the Iraq War, the political unrest in neighboring Syria allowed ISIS to grow in power and in number. Soon, they began taking over land in Syria and began to look toward Iraq.

ISIS, like Al Qaeda, is a jihadist group. The group's goal is to conquer territory and create a fundamentalist Sunni community against nonbelievers, including Shia Muslims, Christians, and Jews. Anyone who does not follow the radical and fundamentalist beliefs of the group, including other Muslims, is targeted. Abu Musab al-Zarqawi, the man who formed Al Qaeda in Iraq during the early stages of the American invasion, is credited with starting ISIS. But Al Qaeda in Iraq suffered many setbacks before becoming very powerful in the region.

In 2006, an American-led airstrike successfully targeted and killed al-Zarqawi. At the time of his death, the group was named Al Qaeda in Iraq. They were weakened following their leader's death and forced out of the country during the surge and the Sunni Awakening. Al Qaeda in Iraq merged with other groups during this time and charged their name to the Islamic State of Iraq (ISI). In 2010, Abu Bakr al-Baghdadi took over as the leader of ISI. This new group grew stronger in Syria as it fought against Syrian president Bashar al-Assad during the civil war. After American troops began to leave Iraq and Prime Minister al-Maliki dissolved the Sunni tribal militias, the group began to carry out more attacks in Iraq. In 2012, al-Baghdadi announced the official return of ISI to Iraq. In 2013, the group changed its name to the Islamic State of Iraq and Syria (ISIS). They now had strongholds in both Iraq and Syria and fought to control new territory.

ISIS showed how powerful they had grown in December 2013, when they took over the city of Fallujah in Iraq. In June 2013, they took over the large city of Mosul. Like Fallujah, Mosul is a large city in the heavily Sunni-populated area of northern Iraq, where large numbers of Baathists and others loyal to Saddam Hussein resided. In June 2014, ISIS declared that it had created a caliphate. The land that they had taken over no longer belonged to either Iraq or Syria. This was their territory now. To reflect the status of their territory, the group renamed itself the Islamic State (IS). This is what they have been known as since then.

By September 2014, IS controlled large territories in both Iraq and Syria. In total, the land IS controls is about the size of the entire United Kingdom. As they gained control over these areas, IS governed residents based on sharia law. Anyone who is not—or does not convert to—Sunni Islam is taxed, exiled, or killed, including Shia Muslims. Women are forced to wear full veils that hide their faces and bodies. Those who go against IS's laws are publicly beheaded. Currently, the Red Cross estimates that ten million people live in Islamic State-controlled territories.[7] It is estimated that there are between 20,000 and 32,000 Islamic State fighters. Disturbingly, thousands of people living around the globe have left their own countries to join the ranks of the Islamic State in Iraq and Syria. Many IS fighters are neither Iraqi nor Syrian. Approximately 250 IS fighters are American.[8]

The Islamic State Attacks

In June 2014, President Obama called for American forces to be sent back into Iraq to fight against IS. That summer, Islamic State fighters captured areas close to the autonomous region of Iraqi Kurdistan. Kurdish leaders grew very fearful. They called upon their allies and the world to help them.

As Islamic State fighters entered into Iraq and captured cities, they committed gross offenses against human rights. In captured northern cities such as Mosul, the houses and businesses of Assyrians and Christians were marked with an Arabic symbol signaling that their owners were marked for extermination and that their belongings could be taken. Assyrians were given the choice to convert to Sunni Islam, pay a *jizya*, or religious tax, flee, or be executed. Many Assyrians fled to autonomous Iraqi Kurdistan, but many more did not have the opportunity.

The Islamic State also targeted Yazidis in order to "cleanse" Iraq of non-Islamic groups. Fleeing execution, groups of Yazidis trekked up mountains near the town of Sinjar in order to seek refuge. There, approximately forty thousand Yazidis, mostly women and children, camped without food or water.[9] They were fearful to descend the mountain and run into Islamic State fighters. Rather than die at the hands of the Islamic State, they were prepared to starve. The persecution and execution of Yazidis in northern Iraq was labeled a genocide by some members of the international community. In response to this, President Obama called for limited airstrikes against the Islamic State. Due to American airstrikes and humanitarian aid, along with the help of peshmerga forces, most of the Yazidis were able to escape from the mountaintops and safely enter into Iraqi Kurdistan.

As airstrikes continued, Islamic State fighters executed captured American, British, and Japanese aid workers and journalists. Videos of these executions were released. People all over the world were outraged by these killings and called for increased military action against the Islamic State. Following this, France, the Netherlands, and Britain decided to join the United States to fight against IS. Soon, Canada, Australia, and Denmark agreed to military intervention against IS as well.

Airstrikes and fighting between coalition and Iraqi forces and the Islamic State continued for many months. In March 2015, al-Baghdadi was reported as being seriously injured in an airstrike. Islamic State forces were reportedly weakened by continued coalition airstrikes. The Iraqi military recaptured the large city of Tikrit that same month. By April 2015, the United States military declared that one-third of all IS territory had been recaptured. This was a major accomplishment for US and coalition forces. However, IS still holds large territories in Syria and smaller territories in Iraq today. In particular, the large city of Ramadi in Iraq fell to IS fighters in May 2015. Battles continue to be fought here between IS fighters and the Iraqi military.

Military intervention seems to be helping in the fight against IS in Iraq and Syria. But the question remains: Will the US military and coalition forces be able to keep fighting IS through airstrikes without "boots on the ground," or more soldiers being sent into Iraq and Syria? After almost nine years of war in Iraq, the American public remains very skeptical about continuing the war with the US military. In fact, President Obama has said multiple times that he will not be sending any more combat troops to Iraq. Recently, however, President Obama announced that he would be sending in special military advisors to help the Iraqi military in their fight against IS. These troops, numbering less than fifty men and women, would train and advise the Iraqis, and provide support as they continue to battle against the Islamic State.

Soon after this announcement, IS claimed responsibility for atrocious attacks against civilians in Lebanon and France. On November 12, 2015, two Islamic State suicide bombers detonated their explosives in a largely Shia neighborhood in southern Beirut. Forty-three people were killed in these attacks. The next day, on November 13, coordinated attacks began in Paris. Islamic State fighters detonated bombs, took hostages, and shot at people in restaurants, bars, and a concert hall. These attacks, and the one in Beirut, were devastating; 129 people were killed in the Paris attacks.[10]

IS has also inspired terrorism in the US. On December 2, 2015, a married couple, Syed Rizwan Farook and his wife Tashfeen Malik, targeted a holiday office party held by the San Bernadino County Office of Public Health. They managed to kill fourteen people and injure twenty-two more before being apprehended by authorities. Both were legal residents of the US (Farook was US-born, and even served in the US Navy). The couple declared that they were motivated by anti-American sentiments preached by IS. IS also inspired another homegrown terrorist, Omar Mateen. On June 12, 2016, Mateen calmly walked into a gay night club in Orlando, FL, and opened fire. This incident is the largest mass shooting in US history, with 49 fatalities and at least 53 injuries (casualty figures as of this printing).

Many politicians and political experts are concerned that the Islamic State will continue to grow in strength unless more drastic action is taken. But thirteen years after entering into a war with Iraq, no one wants to go back. Many people also question whether more war and violence will help the situation. After all, the many years of intervention and war in Iraq hasn't seemed to help. In fact, violence in Iraq is worse now, with the threat of the Islamic Front, than it was during the early years of the Iraq War. As this violence has increased, thousands of refugees have attempted to escape from territory held by the Islamic State in Syria and Iraq. These families have no other choice but to leave their home country and start life anew.

Perhaps the lesson that we should take from the wars in Iraq is that violence always leads to more violence. Instead of calling for more war, even amid our fear and grief, we should remember the lessons of our past and call for more peace.

Chronology

The Persian Gulf War (1990–1991)

1990

August 2: The Persian Gulf War begins when Iraqi troops invade Kuwait.

August 7: Operation Desert Shield begins.

August 8: Saddam Hussein declares that he has annexed Kuwait.

November 29: The United Nations passes Resolution 678, declaring a deadline for Iraqi troops to withdraw from Kuwait before military action.

1991

January 12: The US Congress authorizes military action against Iraq.

January 17: US and coalition airplanes begin airstrikes against Iraqi targets.

February 13: US forces bomb the al-Amiriyah shelter, killing hundreds of Iraqi civilians.

February 24: The ground war begins as US troops enter Iraqi territory.

February 27: US troops enter into Kuwait City.

February 28: President George H.W. Bush announces a cease-fire.

March 3: Iraq accepts the terms of the cease-fire and the war is officially concluded.

The Iraq War (2003–2011)

2003

March 20: The US military begins the invasion of Iraq.

April 10: Baghdad falls to US troops.

May 1: President George W. Bush announces that major combat operations in Iraq are over.

December 13: Saddam Hussein is captured.

2004

March 2: Bombings in Baghdad and Karbala during the Shia festival of Ashura kill hundreds.

March 31: Four American military contractors are killed in Fallujah; the First Battle of Fallujah begins.

April 18: Photos emerge of Iraqi prisoners being abused at Abu Ghraib.

November 7: The Second Battle of Fallujah begins.

2005

January 30: Iraqi parliamentary elections for interim government

November 19: American soldiers in Haditha kill twenty-four Iraqis, including fifteen civilians, following an insurgent attack.

December 15: Iraqi parliamentary elections

2006

February 22: The bombing of the Shia al-Askari mosque leads to increased sectarian violence.

June 7: Abu Musab al-Zarqawi is killed during a US airstrike.

December 30 Saddam Hussein is executed.

2007

January 10: The US troop surge begins.

2010

August 18: US combat troops leave Iraq.

December 17: Arab Spring protests begin and will spread around the Middle East.

2011

December 15: The Iraq War officially ends.

Post US Withdrawal (2011–present)

2014

February: Moqtada al-Sadr declares that he is dissolving the Mahdi Army.

Summer: ISIS captures the city of Mosul. They declare a caliphate and change their name to the Islamic State (IS).

September: The US military begins air raids against the Islamic State.

Chapter Notes

CHAPTER 1. EARLY BEGINNINGS

1. Naomi Shihab Nye, "Interview with Bill Moyers," Retrieved from http://www.pbs.org/now/printable/transcript_nye_print.html.
2. Ryan Chilcote, John King, and Barbara Starr, "U.S. Launches Cruise Missiles at Saddam," www.cnn.com/2003/WORLD/meast/03/19/sprj.irq.main.
3. Charles Kurzman, "Death Tolls of the Iran-Iraq War," October 31, 2013. Retrieved from http://kurzman.unc.edu/death-tolls-of-the-iran-iraq-war.
4. "Gulf War Documents: Meeting between Saddam Hussein and US Ambassador to Iraq April Glaspie," *Global Research*, June 28, 2014, Retrieved from http://www.globalresearch.ca/gulf-war-documents-meeting-between-saddam-hussein-and-ambassador-to-iraq-april-glaspie/31145.
5. Caryle Murphy, "Iraqi Invasion Force Seizes Control of Kuwait," *Washington Post*, August 3, 1990, Retrieved from http://www.washingtonpost.com/wp-srv/inatl/longterm/iraq/timeline/080390.htm.

CHAPTER 2. THE 100-HOUR WAR

1. Ellen Warren et. al, "Bush: 'A Line Has Been Drawn'; Iraq: Kuwait Has Been Annexed President Says Troops' Role Is 'Wholly Defensive,'" *Philly.com*, August 9, 1990, Retrieved from http://articles.philly.com/1990-08-09/news/25932828_1_iraqi-forces-kuwait-saudi-arabia.
2. George Bush, "Address Before a Joint Session of the Congress on the Persian Gulf Crisis and the Federal Budget Deficit,"*The American Presidency Project,* Sept. 11, 1990, http://www.presidency.ucsb.edu/ws/?pid=18820.
3. Department of the Air Force, "White Paper: Air Force Performance in Operation Desert Storm," April 1991, Retrieved from http://www.pbs.org/wgbh/pages/frontline/gulf/appendix/whitepaper.html.

4. "Gulf War Fast Facts," *CNN*, updated November 16, 2015, Retrieved from http://www.cnn.com/2013/09/15/world /meast/gulf-war-fast-facts/.
5. Scott Peterson, "'Smarter' Bombs Still Hit Civilians," *Christian Science Monitor*, October 22, 2002, Retrieved from http://www.csmonitor.com/2002/1022/p01s01-wosc .html.
6. R.W. Apple Jr., "War in the Gulf: Scud Attack; Scud Missile Hits U.S. Barracks, Killing 27," *New York Times*, February 26, 1991, Retrieved from http://www.nytimes.com/1991/ 02/26/world/war-in-the-gulf-scud-attack-scud-missile -hits-a-us-barracks-killing-27.html?_r=0.
7. Remy Melina, "Top 10 Worst Oil Spills," *Live Science*, April 28, 2010, Retrieved from http://www.livescience.com/6363 -top-10-worst-oil-spills.html.
8. PV Hobbs and Radke LF, "Airborne Studies of the Smoke from the Kuwait Oil Fires," *Science*, May 15, 1992, 256(5059):987–91.
9. Craig M. White, *Iraq: The Moral Reckoning* (Lanham, MD: Lexington Books, 2010), p.130.

CHAPTER 3. LEGACY OF THE PERSIAN GULF WAR

1. John and Karl Mueller, "Sanctions of Mass Destruction, "*Foreign Affairs*, May/June, 1999, Retrieved from https:// www.foreignaffairs.com/articles/iraq/1999-05-01/sanctions -mass-destruction.
2. Carl Conetta, "The Wages of War: Iraqi Combatant and Non-Combatant Fatalities in the 2003 Conflict," *Project on Defense Alternatives Research Monograph # 8*, October 20, 2003, Retrieved from http://www.comw.org /pda/0310rm8ap2.html.
3. "70,000 Civilians Died After Gulf War," *The Milwaukee Sentinel*, January 9, 1992, Retrieved from https://news .google.com/newspapers?nid=1368&dat=19920109&id =m4ZQAAAAIBAJ&sjid=1hIEAAAAIBAJ&pg=4491,1537371 &hl=en.
4. *Newsweek*, "Move Forward and Shoot the Things," www .newsweek.com/move-forward-and-shoot-things-201556.
5. Conetta, *Research Monograph # 8*.
6. ibid.

7. "Gulf War," *Saylor.org*, Retrieved from http://www.saylor.org/site/wp-content/uploads/2011/06/Gulf-War.pdf.
8. "World in Brief: Middle East: Gulf War Price Tab Pegged at $61 Billion," *Los Angeles Times*, November 8, 1991, Retrieved from http://articles.latimes.com/1991-11-08/news/mn-950_1_gulf-war.
9. William D. Nordhaus, "The Economic Consequences of a War with Iraq," *Yale University*, November 14, 2002, Retrieved from http://www.econ.yale.edu/~nordhaus/homepage/iraq.pdf.
10. "2003 IRQ: Iraq Watching Briefs — Overview Report, July 2003," Unicef, July 2003, Retrieved from http://www.unicef.org/evaldatabase/index_29697.html.
11. Michael Powell, "The Deaths He Cannot Sanction; Ex-U.N. Worker Details Harm to Iraqi Children," *Washington Post*, December 17, 1998, Retrieved from https://www.high-beam.com/doc/1P2-686609.html.
12. "The World Factbook: Iraq," Central Intelligence Agency, updated November 20, 2015, Retrieved from https://www.cia.gov/library/publications/the-world-factbook/geos/iz.html.
13. Lawrence E. Cline, "The Prospects of the Shia Insurgency Movement in Iraq," *Journal of Conflict Studies*, Vol 20:no 2 (2000), Retrieved from https://journals.lib.unb.ca/inde php/JCS/rt/printerFriendly/4311/4924.
14. *Newsweek.* "Newsweek's Troops in the Persian Gulf," www.newsweek.com/newsweeks-troops-persian-gulf-201548.

CHAPTER 4. STEPS TO THE IRAQ WAR

1. Sean Alfano, "Jimmy Carter Slams Iraq War," CBS News, July 30, 2005, Retrieved from http://www.cbsnews.com/news/jimmy-carter-slams-iraq-war.
2. "September 11th Fast Facts," CNN, updated September 7, 2015, Retrieved from http://www.cnn.com/2013/07/27/us/september-11-anniversary-fast-facts.

3. "CIA's Final Report: No WMDs Found in Iraq," Associated Press, April 25, 2005, Retrieved from http://www.nbcnews.com/id/7634313/ns/world_news-mideast_n_africa/t/cias-final-report-no-wmd-found-iraq/#.VnBvFBorLow.
4. William Clinton, "Full Text of Bill Clinton's Speech to the Labour Party Conference in Blackpool."
5. Noam Chomsky, "The Iraq War and Contempt for Democracy," ZNet, October 31, 2003, Retrieved from http://chomsky.info/20031031.
6. "Largest Anti-War Rally," *Guinness Book of World Records,* Retrieved from http://www.guinnessworldrecords.com/content_pages/record.asp?recordid=54365.
7. Juan Cole, "Falsity of Nuclear Accusation against Iraq Was Known before Bush's Invasion," *Informed Consent*, March 13, 2013, Retrieved from http://www.juancole.com/2013/03/falsity-accusation-invasion.html.
8. Laurence Armand French and Lidija Nikolic-Iovakovic, *War Trauma and its Aftermath: An International Perspective on the Balkan and Gulf Wars,* New York: University Press of America, 2011 (p. 61).

CHAPTER 5. OPERATION IRAQI FREEDOM

1. George W. Bush, "Full Text: George Bush's Speech on the US's Role in Iraq After the Handover," *The Guardian*, May 25, 2004, Retrieved from http://www.theguardian.com/world/2004/may/25/usa.iraq4.
2. "Iraq War in Figures," BBC, December 14, 2011, Retrieved from http://www.bbc.com/news/world-middle-east-11107739.
3. Rory McCarthy, "I am Saddam Hussein the president of Iraq and I Am Willing to Negotiate," *The Guardian*, December 15, 2003, Retrieved from http://www.theguardian.com/world/2003/dec/16/iraq.rorymccarthy.

4. James Wirtz (2007), "The Exquisite Problem of Victory: Measuring Success in Unconventional Operations," In Joseph Cerami and Jay Boggs, *The Interagency and Counterinsurgency Warfare: Aligning and Integrating Military and Civilian Roles in Stability, Security, Transition, and Reconstruction Operations*, Strategic Studies Institute, p. 275.
5. Sharon Otterman, "Iraq: Debaathification," Council on Foreign Relations, April 7, 2005, Retrieved from http://www.cfr.org/iraq/iraq-debaathification/p7853.
6. "The World Factbook: Iraq," Central Intelligence Agency, updated November 20, 2015, Retrieved from https://www.cia.gov/library/publications/the-world-factbook/geos/iz.html.
7. Marc Santora, "Ashura Attacks Leave Dozens Dead in Iraq," *New York Times*, January 30, 2007, Retrieved from http://www.nytimes.com/2007/01/30/world/middleeast/30cnd-iraq.html.

CHAPTER 6. THE WAR INTENSIFIES

1. "A Conversation with Walter Dean Myers About *Sunrise Over Fallujah*," *Scholastic*, 2008, Retrieved from http://www.scholastic.com/teachers/article/conversation-walter-dean-myers-about-sunrise-over-fallujah.
2. Kim Sengupta and Justin Huggler, "Battle for Fallujah Rages," *The Independent*, November 4, 2004, Retrieved from http://www.independent.co.uk/news/world/middle-east/battle-for-fallujah-rages-5350609.html.
3. NPR, "Marine Reflects on Second Battle of Fallujah, 10 Years Later," www.npr.org/2014/11/07/362351981/marine-reflects-on-second-battle-of-fallujah-10-years-later.
4. Mark Seavey, "Battlefields of Terror," *The American Legion Magazine*, August 20, 2015, Retrieved from http://www.legion.org/magazine/229591/battlefields-terror.
5. "Red Cross Estimates 800 Iraqi Civilians Killed in Fallujah,"*Democracy Now*, November 17, 2004, Retrieved from http://www.democracynow.org/2004/11/17/red_cross_estimates_800_iraqi_civilians.

6. "Weekend Wave of Suicide Bombings Kills Dozens," Associated Press, February 20, 2005, Retrieved from http://www.sptimes.com/2005/02/20/news_pf/Worldandnation/Weekend_wave_of_suici.shtml.
7. Liz Sly, "Majority Shiites Win Iraq Vote," *Chicago Tribune*, February 14, 2005, Retrieved from http://articles.baltimoresun.com/2005-02-14/news/0502140270_1_iraq-sunni-shiite.

CHAPTER 7. THE CIVIL CONFLICT AND THE SURGE

1. Rania Azbouzeid, "Al-Sadr Throws Down the Gauntlet on US-Iraq Talks," *Time*, November 14, 2008, Retrived from http://content.time.com/time/world/article/0,8599,1859246,00.html.
2. Tim McGirk, "Collateral Damage or Civilian Massacre in Haditha?" content.time.com/time/world/article/0,8599,1174649,00.html.
3. "Poll Finds Broad Optimism in Iraq, But Also Deep Divisions Among Groups," ABC News, December 12, 2005, Retrieved from https://abcnews.go.com/images/Politics/1000a1IraqWhereThingsStand.pdf.
4. "More than 130 Die, 168 Mosques Attacked in Iraq Violence," *The Daily Star,* February 24, 2006.
5. "2015 UNHCR Country Operations Profile—Iraq," UN Refugee Agency, Retrieved from http://www.unhcr.org/pages/49e486426.html.
6. Marc Santora, James Glanz, and Sabrina Tavernise, "Dictator Who Ruled Iraq with Violence is Hanged for Crimes Against Humanity," www.nytimes.com/2006/12/30/world/middleeast/30hussein.html?_r=0.
7. "Documented Civilian Deaths from Violence," *Iraq Body Count*, Retrieved from https://www.iraqbodycount.org/database.
8. Rachel Martin, "Will The U.S. Win A Second Chance At A Sunni Awakening?" NPR, June 14, 2015, Retrieved from http://www.npr.org/2015/06/14/414334390/will-the-u-s-win-a-second-chance-at-a-sunni-awakening.

CHAPTER 8. AFTER THE WITHDRAWAL, A NEW ENEMY

1. Barack Obama, "Remarks by the President in Address to the Nation on the End of Combat Operations in Iraq," The White House, August 31, 2010, Retrieved from https://www.whitehouse.gov/the-press-office/2010/08/31/remarks-president-address-nation-end-combat-operations-iraq.
2. "US Death Toll in Iraq Hits 4000," CBS, March 23, 2008, Retrieved from http://www.cbsnews.com/news/us-death-toll-in-iraq-hits-4000.
3. "Iraqi deaths from violence 2003–2011," Iraq Body Count, January 2, 2012, Retrieved from https://www.iraqbodycount.org/analysis/numbers/2011/.
4. Margaret Friggis, "Casualties in Iraq: The Human Cost of Occupation," Retrieved from http://antiwar.com/casualties.
5. Priyanka Boghani, "In Their Own Words: Sunnis on their Treatment in Al-Maliki's Iraq," www.pbs.org/wgbh/pages/frontline/iraq-war-on-terror/rise-of-isis/in-their-own-words-sunnis-on-their-treatment-in-al-Malikis-iraq.
6. Mardean Isaac, "The desperate plight of Iraq's Assyrians and other minorities," *The Guardian*, December 24, 2011.
7. Ben Simon,"Red Cross Seeking Permission to Work in IS Territory," AFP, December 6, 2015, Retrieved from http://news.yahoo.com/red-cross-seeking-permission-territory-143414088.html.
8. "What is 'Islamic State'?" BBC, December 2, 2015, Retrieved from http://www.bbc.com/news/world-middle-east-29052144.
9. Martin Chulov, "40,000 Iraqis stranded on mountain as Isis jihadists threaten death," *The Guardian*, August 6, 2014, Retrieved from http://www.theguardian.com/world/2014/aug/07/40000-iraqis-stranded-mountain-isis-death-threat.
10. Lazaro Gamio, Bonnie Berkowitz, and Denise Lu, "What a Year of Islamic State Terror Looks Like," *Washington Post*, November 15, 2015, Retrieved from https://www.washingtonpost.com/graphics/world/islamic-state-attacks.

Glossary

allies— People, states, or countries who group together to form military or political alliances.

annexation—The act of taking over land and declaring it part of one's own country.

caliphate—A form of Islamic government ruled by a leader, called a caliph, of the Muslim community.

communism—A form of government where citizens share common ownership of all goods and means of production.

coup d'état—The overthrow of an established government by a small group of people.

disenfranchised—Those who are not given rights, privileges, or power; the marginalized.

improvised explosive devices (IEDs)—A homemade bomb that is not used by the military, but by terrorist groups, and often placed in roads.

infidels—Those who do not believe in a particular religion or religion more generally.

Islamist group—Groups of conservative and fundamental Muslims, a small number of the Muslim population, who believe in a strict interpretation of the Koran.

jihadist —A person or group or believes in waging armed jihad, or war, against innocent people for political and religious power.

Koran—The holy book of Islam, which is interpreted and followed by Muslims.

pan-Arabism—The belief that Arabs across the Middle East form a community and should become one nation.

radicals—People who have extreme political views that do not follow most of the general population.

sectarianism—Tension or hatred between different sects, or groups, of the same religion.

sharia—Islamic law based on the teachings of the Koran.

Shia Muslims—Members of a branch of Islam who believe that the Prophet Muhammad's son-in-law, Ali, was the rightful successor of Islam following the Prophet's death in 632 AD.

sheikhs—Arab or Muslim leaders of families, villages, or tribes.

Sunni Muslims—Members of a branch of Islam who believe that the Prophet Muhammad's father-in-law, Abu Bakr, was the rightful successor of Islam following the Prophet's death in 632 AD.

weapons of mass destruction (WMDs)—Nuclear, chemical, or biological weapons that can cause mass death.

For More Information

Books

Bingham, Jane. *Living Through the Gulf Wars With Iraq.* Portsmouth, NH: Heinnemann, 2012.

George, Enzo.*The Afghanistan and Iraq Wars: Wars Against Extremism.* New York, NY: Cavendish Square Publishing, 2014.

Pipe, Jim. *Hoping for Peace in Iraq: Divided by Conflict, Wishing for Peace.* Milwaukee, WI: Gareth Stevens Publishing, 2013.

Summers, Elizabeth. *Weapons and Vehicles of the Iraq War.* Mankato, MN: Capstone, 2015.

Websites

Fact Monster: Iraq Primer
www.factmonster.com/spot/iraqprimer1.html
This guide to the Persian Gulf War and the Iraq War provides background information, timelines, and information about the culture of Iraq.

Scholastic News: Rebuilding Iraq
teacher.scholastic.com/scholasticnews/indepth/war-iraq/
This Scholastic website offers a comprehensive and clear history of the war in Iraq.

Videos

"A Look Back at a Decade of Conflict in Iraq" from PBS NewsHour
www.youtube.com/watch?v=BCeAWgGphww
This short video gives basic background information about the Iraq War.

"Understanding the Iraq War" by Daniel Vermilya
study.com/academy/lesson/understanding-the-iraq-war.html
This video is part of a larger lesson on the causes of the Iraq War.

Index

A

Abu Ghraib, 71, 72, 73
al-Assad, Bashar, 102, 103, 106
al-Baghdadi, Abu Bakar, 106, 109
al-Essawi, Rafi, 100, 101
al-Hashemi, Tariq, 101
Al-Jazeera, 80
Allawi, Iyad, 73
allied coalition, 26, 27, 28, 32, 38
al-Maliki, Nouri, 84, 98, 100, 101, 102, 104, 106
al-Qaeda, 49, 50, 52, 53, 71, 83, 89, 93, 94, 95, 101, 103, 104, 106
al-Sadr, Muqtada, 69, 70
al-Zarqawi, Abu Musab, 71, 105, 106
American Air Force, 25, 27, 38
American Special Forces, 28
an-Anfal Campaign, 15, 39, 54
Aramaic, 9, 103
Ashura, 71
Askariyya, 88, 89

B

Baath party, 12, 13, 14, 68, 73, 77
Baghdad, Iraq, 13, 14, 27, 30, 48, 57, 59, 60, 61, 62, 63, 66, 67, 69, 71, 88, 90, 93, 100
Bakr, Ahmed Hassan, 13
bin Laden, Osama, 49, 53
Blair, Tony, 51
Bouazizi, Mohamed, 102
British Broadcasting Corporation (BBC), 80
Bush, George H.W., 8, 19, 24, 25, 26, 32, 48
Bush, George W., 8, 48, 50, 51, 55, 56, 62, 63, 91

C

Central Intelligence Agency (CIA), 12
Cheney, Dick, 24, 52, 55
Chirac, Jacques, 51
Chomsky, Noam, 80
Clifton, Tony, 38, 44
Clinton, William, 47, 48, 52
Coalition Provisional Authority (CPA), 65, 66, 68, 104

D

Dean, Howard, 54
Defense Intelligence Agency, 55

E

economic losses, 38-39
economic sanctions, 20-21, 39, 40, 41
effects of sanctions, 41-42

F

Fallujah, Iraq, 73, 74, 77, 78, 79, 80, 81, 106
Fedayeen Saddam, 60, 61, 65
Feingold, Russ, 54
Fertile Crescent, 9
First Battle of Fallujah, 74, 77
14 July Revolution, 11, 12
Franks, Tommy, 56

G

Glaspie, April, 19
Green Zone, 65

H

Haditha, Iraq, 87, 88

Halliday, Denis, 41
Hussein Saddam, 8, 10, 13, 14, 15, 17, 18, 19, 21, 23, 24, 26, 27, 28, 31, 32, 39, 41, 42, 43, 44, 47, 48, 49, 50, 51, 52, 54, 56, 57, 59, 60, 61, 62, 63, 65, 66, 67, 71, 73, 77, 83, 90, 91, 106
Hussein, Qusay, 57
Hussein, Uday, 57

I

improvised explosive devices (IEDs), 69, 78, 79
International Mission for Iraqi Elections, 83
Iran-Iraq War, 17, 18, 39
Iraq, history of, 9-15
Iraqi Air Force, 28
Islamic Front, 111
Islamic State (IS), 107, 108, 109, 110, 111
Islamic State of Iraq (ISI), 106
Islamic State of Iraq and Syria (ISIS), 104, 105

J

jizya, 108
Jolan District, 79

K

Karbala, 71
Kennedy, Edward, 54
Kurds, 43
Kuwait, 18, 19, 20, 21, 23, 24, 25, 26, 27, 28, 31, 32, 35, 39, 44, 47, 57, 59, 60

L

Libya, 102

M

Mahajan, Rahul, 80
Mahdi Army, 69, 70
McKirk, Tim, 88
Middle East, 12, 24, 102

N

New Way Forward, The, 91
Newsweek, 38
Nichols, Greg, 78

O

Obama, Barack, 98, 99
Operation Desert Fox, 44
Operation Desert Sabre, 28
Operation Desert Storm, 26
Operation Iraqi Freedom, 57
Operation Phantom Fury, 74
Ottoman Empire, 10-11, 18
Oval Office, 99

P

Pentagon, 49
Persian Gulf oil spill, 30-31
Powell, Colin, 51, 55, 56

Q

Qasim, Abd al-Karim, 11, 12, 13, 14

R

Red Cross, 79
Rice, Condoleeza, 55
Rumsfeld, Donald, 55

S

Sabah, Sheikh, 20
Saudi Arabia, 9, 20, 24, 26, 28, 30, 49
Schwarzkopf, Norman, 25, 32

Second Battle of Fallujah, 74, 77, 79, 80, 81
sharia law, 107
Shia Muslims, 43, 48
Sons of Iraq, 95, 98, 101
Sunni Awakening, 93, 95, 98, 106
Sunni Muslims, 67, 69, 73, 83, 84, 88, 89, 91, 93, 94, 95, 98, 100, 101, 102, 103, 104, 106, 107, 108
Syria, 102, 103, 104, 105, 106, 107, 109, 110, 111

T

Taliban, 49
Terazzas, Miguel, 87
Time magazine, 88

U

UNICEF, 41
United Nations, 20, 23, 47, 48, 54, 89
United States Congress, 25, 26, 38
United States Senate, 50
UN Security Council, 26, 32, 33, 56, 57
US Army, 61

W

weapons of mass destruction (WMDs), 50, 51, 54, 55, 56
World Trade Center, 49
World War I, 11
World War II, 12